William Henry Giles Kingston

The Two Whalers or Adventures in the Pacific

William Henry Giles Kingston

The Two Whalers or Adventures in the Pacific

ISBN/EAN: 9783337177942

Printed in Europe, USA, Canada, Australia, Japan

Cover: Foto ©Andreas Hilbeck / pixelio.de

More available books at **www.hansebooks.com**

THE TWO WHALERS;

OR,

Adventures in the Pacific.

BY

WILLIAM H. G. KINGSTON,

Author of "*Ned Garth*," "*Owen Hartley*," *&c.*, *&c.*

PUBLISHED UNDER THE DIRECTION OF
THE COMMITTEE OF GENERAL LITERATURE AND EDUCATION,
APPOINTED BY THE SOCIETY FOR PROMOTING
CHRISTIAN KNOWLEDGE.

LONDON:
SOCIETY FOR PROMOTING CHRISTIAN KNOWLEDGE,
NORTHUMBERLAND AVENUE, CHARING CROSS, W.C. ;
43, QUEEN VICTORIA STREET, E.C.
BRIGHTON: 135, NORTH STREET.
NEW YORK: E. & J. B. YOUNG & CO.

"It darted off along the surface at a rapid rate."

THE TWO WHALERS.

CHAPTER I.

I HAIL from Deal, where my father was highly respected, not on account of his worldly wealth, for of that he had but small store, but because he was an honest, upright, God-fearing man, who did his duty to his neighbour, and ruled his family with discretion.

And my mother—she was a mother!—so loving and gentle and considerate; she kept us, her children, of whom there were nine, I being the third, in excellent order, and yet we scarcely discovered the means she employed. We trusted her implicitly ; we knew that she entered into all our sorrows as well as into our joys and amusements. How carefully she bound up a cut finger or bathed a bruised knee ; or if we were trying to manufacture any toy, how ready she was to show us the best way to do the work ; how warmly she admired it when finished, and how proudly she showed it to father when he came in.

I was accustomed from my earliest days to the sight of ships coming into or going out of the Downs, or brought up before our town, and I used to listen with deep interest to the account of his adventures in all parts of the world with which our neighbour, Captain Bland, was wont to entertain us when he came to our house, or when we went in to take tea with him and Mrs. Bland and their daughter Mary. I can, therefore, scarcely remember the time when I did not wish to become a sailor, though as my eldest brother Bill was intended for the sea, and indeed went away when I was still a little fellow, my father had thoughts of bringing me up to some trade or other. I should have been content to follow my father's wishes, or rather to have done what he believed best for me, had I been sent away inland, where I could not have heard nautical matters talked about, and where the sea and shipping would have been out of my sight. While I remained at home the desire grew stronger and stronger to become like the sea-faring men I was constantly meeting—pilots, masters and mates, and boatmen—and I may venture to say that a finer race of sailors are nowhere to be found than those belonging to Deal.

Captain Bland was a thorough sailor. He dearly loved the sea, and the ship he commanded, and his crew—at least he took a warm interest in their welfare—but he loved his wife and daughter more, and for their sakes he remained on shore longer than he would otherwise have done. Still, he made three or four voyages while I was a youngster, and he always spoke as if he had no intention of abandoning the sea until he had laid by a competency for old age. How many a master says the same, and goes on ploughing the ocean in the delusive hope of reaping a harvest till the great reaper gathers him into his garner.

Notwithstanding my predilections in favour of a sea life, I was still undecided as to my future career, when one winter's day, after school hours, as I was taking a run out on the London Road, I saw coming along towards me a fine broad, well-built lad, with a sun-burnt countenance, and a stick having a bundle at the end of it over his shoulder. His dress, and the jaunty way he walked, with a slight roll, as if trying to steady himself on a tossing deck, showed me that he was a sailor. We were going to pass each other, when he looked hard at me, and I looked hard at him. Suddenly it struck me that I knew his features; so I stopped, and he stopped, and we gazed into one another's faces.

"Can you be brother Bill?" I exclaimed.

"Bill's my name, my hearty. And you!—are you brother Jack? Yes, I'm sure you are!" And grasping my hand he wrung it till I thought he would have wrung it off, while, half-laughing, half-crying for pleasure, he asked, "How's father and mother, and Susan and Jane, and Mary and Dick, and the rest of them; and little Tommy?"

He was the youngest of us, and could just toddle when Bill went away. Thus he ran on, asking qustion after question, which I answered as well as I could, while we went towards home at a pretty round trot—he eager to get there and see them all again, and I almost as eager to have the satisfaction of rushing in and shouting out, "Here's Bill come back again!"

I need not describe the way Bill was received. No one seemed to think that they could make enough of him. Mary, a small girl, sat on his knee at supper, with one arm round his neck, and ever and anon gave him a kiss and a hug, exclaiming, "Dear Bill, we are so glad you're come back;" and Susan and Jane placed themselves one on each side that they might the better help him to what was on the table; and we bigger boys listened eagerly to all he said; and father watched him with pride, and the light shone brighter than ever from mother's eyes as she gazed at him; and little Tommy came toddling into the room in his night-gown (having scrambled out of his crib) saying, "Tommy want see dat brodder Bill really come home—all right—dere he is—hurrah!" and off he ran again with Susan at his heels, but he had nimbly climbed into his nest before she caught him.

As to myself, I looked at Bill with unbounded admiration, and eagerly listened to every word which dropped from his lips. He had plenty to talk about, and wonders of all sorts to describe, for he had been in the Indian Sea, and visited China, and the west coast of America, and several islands in the Pacific, and gone round the world. How he rattled on! I thought Drake, Cavendish, and Dampier, Lord Anson and Captain Cook were nothing to him—at all events, that I would far rather hear the narrative of his adventures than read theirs.

I was almost vexed with Captain Bland for coming in one evening, even though Mary accompanied him, because Bill became suddenly far more reticent than usual in his presence, if not altogether dumb, and when he did speak, merely described in a modest tone some very commonplace occurrences. I could not make it out. After some time, when Bill was out of ear-shot, I heard Captain Bland remark to father that he liked lads who did not speak about themselves. It was a pretty sure sign that they were better doers than talkers. " He'll succeed, will that lad of yours; he's kept his eyes open wherever he's been; he'll make a smart officer one of these days," he added.

I was much pleased when Captain Bland thus spoke of Bill, and I thought to myself, what would he have said if he had heard him describe some of the wonderful adventures he had narrated to us. When I afterwards told Bill what the old captain had said, and my ideas on the subject, he laughed heartily.

"Why, Jack, he would have shut me up pretty smartly," he answered. "Old cocks don't allow young ones to crow in their presence."

Bill made ample amends for his previous silence when we were together, knowing that I was never tired of listening to him. I could think about nothing else but what he had told me, and I made up my mind that I would far rather become a sailor than follow any other calling. I told him so.

"Well, Jack, I think you're right," he said; "I wouldn't change if I had the offer—no, not to become Prime Minister of England or the first merchant in the land. Remember, though, it isn't all smooth sailing. You must expect rough weather as well as fine; but if you're determined to go I'll speak to father, and I don't think that he'll refuse you."

Bill fulfilled his promise, and father, after consulting Captain Bland, agreed to let me go, provided I was of the same mind when I was old enough to be apprenticed. Neither our mother nor our sisters had a word to say against my wishes; nor had Mary Bland.

"I wish that I was a boy, Jack, that I might go also," she exclaimed. "We shall be very, very sorry to lose you," she added after a short silence; "but then, you know, you will come back, and how glad we all shall be to see you again."

Bill told me how well pleased he was that father had given me leave to go to sea. "But I want you to study navigation at once, so that you may become an officer as soon as possible. You'll never get on without that," he said, and producing an old, well-thumbed edition of Hamilton Moore's " Epitome of Navigation," he added, " I 'll give you this, Jack. It has served me, and will serve you well if you master it as I 've done."

How I did prize that book! I doubt if I ever valued anything more in my life. My brother, I should have said, had been at an excellent nautical school in Deal, established a few years before by several officers of the Royal Navy, where he gained much credit by his intelligence and attention to his studies. As soon as it was finally settled that I was to go to sea I was sent to the same school on the day my brother left home to go on his next voyage. I easily passed in, as I knew all the simple rules of arithmetic thoroughly, and was pretty well up in decimals. Having learned from my brother that the use of logarithms and the first principles of geometry would soon be taught me at school, with his help I had at once set to work on them, and after he went away I continued my studies in the evenings when other boys were at play, so that I quickly mastered all those necessary preliminaries. I consequently got over them at school with a rapidity which astonished the master, and with no little pride I heard the inspector, a naval captain, remark, " First-rate boy—beats his brother—be a master in a jiffy."

The result of my working so hard out of hours was that at our annual examination I took the first prize, and was shortly afterwards pronounced fit to be sent to sea. As I still held to my wish to go, my father at once wrote to the owners of several first-class South Sea whalers, who immediately agreed to send me as an apprentice on board one of their ships, the "Eagle," Captain Hake, just about to sail for the Pacific.

On the night before my departure I slept but little for thinking of the novel and wonderful scenes I expected to go through, and I am pretty sure that my kind mother did not close her eyes, but from a different cause. She was thinking of parting from me, and of the dangers to which I was to be exposed. She was praying that I might be preserved from them I know, for she told me so. At three o'clock in the morning she called me up, that I might be ready to start with my father by the mail coach for Margate, whence we were to go up the river to London by steamer. How earnestly did my pious father at family prayers, which he never omitted, commend me to the care of Him who watches over all the creatures of His hands! I felt that there was a reality in that prayer, such as I had never before comprehended.

Breakfast over, and parting embraces given,

we started, and rattling away to Margate, were soon on board the " Royal Adelaide " on our way up the Thames. Bitter as was the cold, I was too much occupied in running about and examining everything connected with the steamer to mind it. The helm, the machinery, the masts and rigging, the huge paddle-wheels, the lead and lead-line, all came under my notice. As I was in no ways bashful I made the acquaintance of several persons on board, and among others I spoke to a lad considerably my senior, whose dress and well-bronzed face and hands showed me that he was a sailor.

"Are you going to sea, youngster?" he asked, looking me over from head to foot, as if to judge how far I was cut out for a nautical life.

"Yes, in a few days, I hope, on board the ' Eagle,'" I answered.

"That is curious; she is the ship I belong to," he remarked. "You're in luck, for she's a smart craft, and, as things go, we are tolerably comfortable on board; but you must be prepared to take the rough with the smooth, mind you; there are a good many things to rub against afloat as well as ashore, you 'll find."

"And what sort of man is the captain?" I asked somewhat eagerly, anxious to know the character of my future commander

" The captain is the captain, and while you are on board his ship you'd better not rub against him, but listen to what he tells you to do, and do it; sharp's the word with him." I was not much the wiser from this information, but I gathered from it that Captain Hake was a man who would stand no nonsense. I determined at all events to learn my duty, and to try and perform it to the best of my power. I next asked my new friend his name, supposing that, though he looked young, he might be one of the mates.

"Andrew Medley," he answered. "I am still an apprentice, as you are about to become, so we shall be messmates; and if you are wise, I hope that we shall get on well together."

"I hope so," I replied, with confidence, liking his looks. Just then my father came up, and hearing that Medley was to be my messmate, shook hands with him. Presently he sent me off on some excuse or other, and drawing Medley aside, had a short, earnest talk with him. What it was about I did not at the time know.

"I am thankful that you have got so right-minded a young man for a messmate," observed my father shortly afterwards. "He will, I hope, prove a true friend to you."

I must not stop to describe my astonishment at the crowded thoroughfares we passed along on our way to the inn where we lodged for the night. The next morning we went to the office of the owners in Old Broad Street, where I was, by the signing of certain papers, bound apprentice for four years on board the good ship "Eagle," South Sea whaler, Captain Hake commander. This done, we made our way to the river, and getting into a wherry proceeded in her to the dock, in which my ship lay getting ready for sea. On going on board I looked round for Medley, but could nowhere see him, and presently my father took me up to Captain Hake, who was standing aft, giving his orders in a sharp, ringing voice, which showed that he was accustomed to be obeyed.

"If he is the man his appearance betokens, he is a very fine fellow indeed," I thought to myself. He was of good height, with broad shoulders, an open countenance, well bronzed, large blue eyes, and a thick bushy beard. I don't know if he formed as good an opinion of me as I did of him, but he looked down good-naturedly as he said, "I'll do my best to make a seaman of the lad, Mr. Kemp, and I'll keep an eye on him, as I do on all the youngsters under my charge."

He then invited us into the cabin and gave us some luncheon, after which my father took his leave. I accompanied him to the side. Pressing my hand, with a trembling voice he said, "We may never meet again, Jack. You have chosen a perilous profession, and may at any moment be called away ; but, my dear boy, seek always so to live that you may be ready to go when summoned."

I watched him as he pulled away till his wherry was lost to sight among the shipping, and at first felt very sad ; but I soon recovered my spirits, and having got one of the few seamen who had joined to stow my chest away for me on the half deck, where he told me the apprentices slept, I set out to make an exploring expedition round the ship. I should have been wiser had I waited for Medley, or, at all events, avoided touching anything with the use of which I was not acquainted.

Among other novelties which I examined was the windlass, which had the handles shipped, but I did not observe that on the top of it was coiled a large quantity of iron chain out of the way to allow of the deck being scraped. I saw that the big thing was intended to go round, so I thought that I would try if I could move it by myself. I pressed with all my force against one of the handles, when, to my infinite satisfaction, the windlass began to revolve, but as it did so, to my

B

still greater dismay, down came the chain rattling on to the deck. In vain I tried to stop it. I then made a desperate effort to replace it, but as it had taken probably two men some time to put it up I had not the slightest chance of succeeding. My task was something like that of Sisyphus, a man of ancient days, who had to roll a huge stone to the top of a mountain, but which always came down again as soon as he got it there.

I had not been long engaged in my hopeless undertaking when my ears were assailed by such a volley of abuse as I had never before heard in my life. As I turned round, letting go the chain, which came rattling down again on deck, I discovered that it proceeded from a head that had suddenly appeared above the combings of the fore hatch. It might have been a picturesque head, but was not pleasant-looking to my eyes. On the top was an old party-coloured nightcap, beneath which stuck out on all sides a mass of reddish hair resembling oakum or shavings, as untwisted rope is called at sea ; a pair of ferrety eyes, a snub nose, and a huge mouth half concealed by a bushy beard, completed the countenance of the individual who was addressing me. I need not repeat what he said, but if his remarks were true I was among the greatest reprobates this evil world has ever produced. I stood with my hands by my side mutely gazing at him, for I had nothing to say for myself. I was conscious that I had done something wrong, though not meriting the remarks to which I was listening.

"Arrah, now spake, youngster, if you've a tongue belonging to you," cried the head. Still I said nothing. Presently, below the head a pair of broad shoulders covered with a red shirt emerged from the hatchway, and I had an unpleasant vision of a bear-like hand grasping a short piece of knotted rope. The next instant a short thick-set man in tarry trousers springing on deck advanced towards me, ominously flourishing the piece of rope. I did not think of running, for I had nowhere to run to, so I stood stock still. Down came the rope on my shoulders. I tried hard not to cry out. A second and a third blow followed. I had on a pretty thick jacket on account of the cold, so that I was not so much hurt as I might have been; still, as I did not like the treatment I was receiving, I tried to get out of my tormentor's way, and in doing so fell over the chain flat on the deck, striking my nose in a way which made the blood flow pretty quickly. He not noticing this gave me another whack, which hurt more than all the others, as it was on the part most exposed, and was about to repeat it, when I heard a voice say

"Hold fast there, Dan ; enough of that. The boy hasn't been on board an hour and you must needs get foul of him."

"Who are you that's afther spakin' to me in that way? Sure, if I'm not mighty mistaken, you're only an apprentice yourself," exclaimed Dan, in an angry tone.

While he was speaking I crawled along the deck out of his way, and looking up, I recognised my acquaintance on board the steamer, Andrew Medley, who replied calmly, "Whether or not I am only an apprentice, I'll not stand by and see a young boy ill-treated who hasn't strength to defend himself."

The ruffian laughed hoarsely, but when he saw the blood streaming down my face as Medley assisted me to get up, he looked somewhat alarmed, for he remembered that we were not yet at sea, and that although he might then treat me much worse with impunity it would be prudent to avoid the risk of being summoned before a magistrate for an assault.

"Are you much hurt, Jack?" asked Medley, as he led me aft.

"Only my nose bleeds ; though the last cuts that man gave me were not pleasant," I replied.

"If that's all, come below and we'll soon get you set to rights with some cold water," said

Medley. " I am glad I came in time to save you from tasting more of Dan Hogan's colt. Though a bully, he is a good boat-steerer, so the captain keeps him on, but, for my part, I think the ship would be better without him."

" I should have been so, at all events, just now," I remarked, and I went down with Medley to the half-deck.

With the help of a sponge and some cold water I was soon put to rights, and except that I felt an unpleasant sensation in the back I was not much the worse for the beating I had received. The first mate, Mr. Renshaw, however, who had heard of my performance from Hogan, quickly sent for me, and after scolding me for my care-lessness, ordered me to draw a bucket of water. " I'll find something for you to do, depend on that, youngster," he observed, and he was as good as his word.

I was not over successful in carrying out this my first piece of duty, for in attempting to secure a rope to the bucket that I might lower it over the side, I made a slippery hitch. To my dismay when I hauled in the rope the bucket was not at the end. It had gone to the bottom. I fully expected to get another taste of Dan Hogan's colt, but Medley, who at that moment came on deck, seeing what had happened, lowered a hook and fished up the bucket. He then showed me how to make a proper hitch, and the mate kept me drawing water till my arms ached.

I was feeling very hungry, and was wondering if I should get any dinner, when Medley told me that no fires were allowed to be lighted on board, and consequently that no cooking could be carried on while the ship was in dock. I was thinking of petitioning the steward for some bread and cheese, when the captain came out of his cabin and told me to accompany him on shore. Before long we stopped close to the dock entrance, at the well-known inn, "The Dog and Duck," and taking me to the landlady told her to supply me with whatever I wanted to eat and drink. I thanked him very much as he left me there, and the hostess asking me if I should like something at once, to which I replied, "I should think so indeed," speedily placed a capital dinner before me. I did not fail after this, whenever I felt hungry, to pay a visit to "The Dog and Duck," not being particular as to hours, and mine hostess always looked glad to see me.

I had learned the names of the masts and yards and ropes, and a good deal besides, thanks to Medley's assistance, by the time the ship was ready for sea. Even Dan Hogan readily told me anything I wanted to know, and seemed as pleased as his rough nature would allow that I did not show any ill-feeling towards him on account of the drubbing he had given me. In about a week after I went on board we hauled out of dock, and a tug towed us down to Gravesend. Here the owner paid us a parting visit, followed by the Jew slop-sellers, with whom the men spent most of their advanced wages in the purchase of all sorts of articles, the more prudent furnishing themselves with warm clothing, and also with knives and trinkets to barter with the natives of the islands we were likely to visit.

The following day we reached the Nore lightship, where, the weather looking dirty, by the orders of the pilot who had charge of us we brought up. Scarcely was the anchor at the bottom and the hands were aloft furling sails than down came the gale upon us. The pilot, a jolly old fellow, kept singing out, "More yet, more yet," meaning that we were to veer away more cable, and he did not seem satisfied till the whole of it was out. From this circumstance the men called him "Old More Yet." I forget his real name. I was thus early in my sea life to learn what a real gale of wind is like.

CHAPTER II.

E lay at the Nore for several days with our bows pitching into the sea and the spray flying over us, and after all, having lost both anchor-stocks, and received other damage, we were obliged to return to Gravesend to get them repaired. This done, we again sailed.

Light winds prevailing, we were some time getting clear of the river. We thought that we should at once stand down channel, but as we rounded the North Foreland the weather looked more threatening than ever, and we found that we were to bring up in the Downs. I by this time had not only got my sea legs, but was pretty handy aloft. The winds being contrary we had to tack ship very frequently. I saw the first mate looking up, when just then he sang out to me, "Away there, Jack, and clear that rope from the lee fore-yard arm." I knew what he wanted me to do, so running up the rigging, lay out on the yard, and quickly performed the duty required of me. Instead, however, of returning at once on deck, I sat watching several other ships beating up to an anchorage, as we were, while I did not hear "Old More Yet," the pilot, give the order "about ship." Suddenly I felt the yard beginning to swing round. In another instant I should have been hurled off as from a catapult into the seething ocean, or been dashed on the deck.

There was but one thing to do. Retaining my presence of mind, I made a desperate spring and caught hold of the topmast backstay, down which I was sliding to the rail, when I saw the first mate rushing forward to try and catch me as I fell, he having just recollected that he had sent me aloft. His countenance expressed the greatest alarm, for he was a kind-hearted man, and fully believed that I should have been killed or terribly injured. When he saw that I was safe he rated me soundly for my carelessness, and told me never to play the same trick again. I saw, however, that he was not really angry, and I fancy that I gained some credit with him by the way I had sprung on to the backstay. Had I missed it I should have been dashed to pieces.

At length we brought up in the Downs, with

two anchors down, the wind blowing a heavy gale at south-west. The sea was the colour of pea-soup, tumbling and foaming and hissing, the wind roared and whistled through the rigging, and ships were driving in all directions—some threatening to come down upon us. To be ready for any emergency the hands were kept on deck, and "Old More Yet" stood with his keen eyes watching them, prepared to give the order to veer away the cables should it be necessary. We escaped all accidents, however, and the weather began to moderate.

The captain or the mates found employment for me from morning till night. I was indeed, as the youngest on board, at every one's beck and call; but I did not complain. I had come to sea to do my duty, and I knew that that was to obey those over me in all things lawful. One of my tasks was to keep the captain's cabin in order. I was one day engaged in sweeping it when I heard outside a voice I knew. It was my father's. He looked somewhat surprised at finding me thus employed, but at once saw that I took it as a matter of course, and was in good heart. My younger brother Dick was with him. I was very glad to see them, and having finished my job I asked them to come down on the half deck, where, while they were seated on Medley's and my chests, I regaled them with bread and cheese.

"Won't you give it up and come on shore with us?" asked Dick, thinking that I must be leading a very hard life.

"No, thank you," I answered. "Matters are improving. I got a thrashing the first day and have never had one since. It has been blowing pretty hard till now, but we shall have fine weather in time, and I shall like the life very well. It is better to begin with the rough and to end with the smooth than the other way."

"Rightly said, Jack," observed my father, well pleased to see me so contented.

I sent many loving messages to my mother and sisters, not forgetting Mary and Captain Bland, and after he had had a short conversation with Medley and another with the captain he returned on shore. I felt somewhat sad while I watched him and Dick as they pulled away, and had I then been asked to go with them I should have said yes; however, the feeling soon wore off and I went on with my ordinary duties as if home and all I held dear were not almost in sight.

Again we were under weigh, but it came on to blow as hard as ever from the old quarter. Still we kept at it, beating down channel with the seas breaking over our bows. I was just going along the deck with some of the cabin dinner when, the ship diving into a heavier sea than usual, I found myself washed clean over the windlass, a piece of boiled beef flying in one direction, a dumpling in another, and potatoes and turnips scattered on every side. I rushed here and there to save as many as I could, and, helped by the cook and Medley, I collected the greater portion, but the captain looked very blue when I placed the food all cold and sodden on the table. It spoke well for him that he did not blow me up; but he knew that it was not from my fault that his dinner was spoilt, and I dare say that the same thing had occurred to him when he was a youngster.

I had just returned on deck, where the first mate, shouting "Helm's alee!" was in the act of putting the ship about, when, as I was going forward, I saw Medley with two other men, one of whom was John Major, an ordinary seaman, standing a short distance from me. Suddenly I heard a dull thud as if a heavy blow had been struck, followed by a piercing shriek. The clew of the mainsail was lashing about wildly in the gale. I saw a body lifted from the deck and carried over the bulwarks. It was but a momentary glimpse. I could scarcely have told whether or not it was a human being I had seen till I looked towards where the three persons had been standing. One was gone. The mate instantly hove the ship up into the wind, a grating and some spars were thrown overboard, and the captain, rushing on deck, ordered a boat to be lowered. Notwithstanding the dangerously heavy sea running a willing crew, with the second mate, jumped into her. Not seeing Medley I ran to the side, fearing that he was the victim. I saw the grating and spars, but could nowhere perceive a man's head amid the foaming billows. I expected every moment as I watched the boat tumbling and tossing about that she would be swamped. The captain and first mate were looking anxiously towards the place where the poor fellow must have fallen, but their countenances showed that they did not see him.

"He's lost, I fear," said a voice near me. I turned and saw Medley by my side. I was greatly relieved.

"Who has gone?" I asked.

"John Major," he answered. "He was speaking to me at the moment."

"Very awful," I remarked, "so suddenly to be called out of the world."

"Remember, Jack, that either you or I may be as suddenly summoned to meet our God.

We must so live as to be prepared," he answered solemnly.

The boat, the search in vain, now coming alongside was hoisted up, and the ship kept on her course. Scarcely, however, had the yards been braced round than down came the gale upon us with far greater force than before. There was no use longer contending against it. The helm was put up and we ran—tearing through the water—back again into the Downs. Here we lay day after day waiting for a fair wind. It was much the same to me, but a severe trial of temper to the captain and most of the ship's company, who wanted to be in the Pacific catching whales.

I have not yet described the crew of the "Eagle." There was the captain, three mates, the carpenter and his mate, the cooper and his mate, the armourer, steward and cook, four boat-steerers, four able seamen, eight ordinary seamen, the doctor, and two apprentices—namely, Medley and I. The ship was thus strongly manned for her size, but in the whaling service, when sometimes four boats are away at a time, a large number of hands are required.

By the time we had been a week in the Downs a fleet of some hundred merchantmen were collected there, driven in by the long continuing

south-westerly gales. We had very little com-
munication with the shore, though I managed to
send a letter home, and Medley wrote to his
friends.

"Never miss an opportunity of writing home,
Jack," he said to me ; "I know the pleasure it
gives to those who love us to receive a letter,
and the anxiety they suffer when they have to
go long without hearing from us."

I followed his advice, and wrote by every
homeward bound ship we fell in with, though
many of my letters did not reach their destination. We also got a man, Eben Dredge, in place
of poor John Major lost overboard. Still the
south-wester blustered and roared. Some of the
men declared that it had set in for good, and
that there never would be any other wind as long
as the world lasted.

At length one morning when Medley and I
were below, we heard the first mate shouting, "All
hands up anchor! Fair wind, boys! Be smart
there, all of you." We sprang on deck. The
watch below came tumbling up with eager looks.
The wind had suddenly veered round to the
east-north-east. Every man, including the cook
and steward, set to work with a will ; while some
with a cheery song hove round the windlass,
others flew aloft to loose sails. Hundreds of

ships were setting sail at the same time, their white canvas rapidly expanding to the breeze.

We were among the first to get under weigh, and running past numerous ships we took the lead and kept it, closely pressed, however, by another whaler, the " Fair Rosamond," but we lost sight of her off the Isle of Wight. As if the " Eagle " was eager to make up for lost time she ran under every stitch of canvas she could carry at the rate of nearly twelve knots an hour to the Lizard, when the wind fell ; but it breezed up again when we were in the Bay of Biscay, and blew great guns and small arms, as sailors say, or in other words, very nearly a hurricane. I own that I did not like it. Our stout ship looked like a mere cockle-shell amid the mighty billows, which in huge watery walls rose half-way up the masts, threatening every instant to overwhelm her. Though I tried to conceal my fears Medley detected them, but he did not laugh at me.

" I once should have felt as you do, Jack, but I know that we are as safe here in God's hands as on shore," he observed. " Our ship is well built, well found, and well manned, and I trust that we shall weather this gale, and any others we may have to encounter."

We did weather it without carrying away a

rope-yarn, and having sighted Madeira steered for the Cape de Verde Islands, at one of which, Brava, we called to obtain fresh provisions and to ship several tall Kroomen to pull the midship oars in the whale boats. Very fine fellows they were, with gentle, happy dispositions, never grumbling or complaining, and they were consequently much liked by the officers and all the best men of the crew.

After crossing the line " Sail ho ! " was shouted from the masthead. We steered towards her. The stranger proved to be an English brig bound from Brazil to Liverpool. The wind being light our captains exchanged visits, and Medley, I, and others wrote home by her. When in the latitude of the River Plate preparations were made for bad weather, as the winter of that region was approaching. The long royal-masts were sent down and replaced by stump topgallant masts, the flying jib-boom, and the studding-sail booms were also sent down, and all the boats, except one, were got in and secured, and the hatches were battened down, and everything else was done to make the ship light aloft. Some of the men thought the captain over careful, but it was soon shown that he was right.

" We shall have it before long, thick and strong," I heard him remark to the first mate,

C

though at the time there was scarcely a breath of wind. "We'll stow the mainsail, and close reef the topsails."

"Aye, aye, sir," answered the mate, and the hands were sent aloft to perform the operation. Still an hour or more passed away, and we continued on our course.

"The old man is croaking again," growled out Dan Hogan.

"Belay the slack there, mate. The captain keeps his weather eye open, which is more than some aboard this ship do," said Eben Dredge. "What do you think of those black clouds out there?"

"Maybe there's a little wind in them," answered Hogan.

"A little do you say!" exclaimed Dredge. "See, here it comes to show us whether there's a little or not."

As he spoke the wind struck the ship like the blow of a mighty hammer right ahead. She gathered stern way and some of the after dead-lights being open the cabin was half filled with water. Had we been under more sail, the ship might possibly have gone down or her masts would have been carried away. I rushed forward to call the carpenter and his mate, and we soon had the dead-lights closed. While I was afterwards engaged with the steward in swabbing up the cabin and putting things to rights we felt the ship give some tremendous rolls.

"Hillo! what for come ober her now?" exclaimed Domingo, my companion, who was a black.

On going on deck I found that she had fallen off into the trough of the sea, and was being sent from side to side in a way which seemed sufficient to jerk the masts out of her. The rigging was well set up, or they would have gone to a certainty. We had not seen the worst of it. The gale blew harder and harder, and presently down came the rain in a way I had never seen it fall before, in regular torrents, as if some huge reservoirs had been emptied out on us in a moment, flooding the decks, and wetting us through our pea-coats to the skin.

Though several accidents happened we weathered this our first real gale, and I found that the one we had encountered in the Bay of Biscay was scarcely worthy of the name of a gale. Sail being again made, we stood southward, till at the end of April we sighted Cape Horn, and the hopes of all were raised that we should soon be round it; but not half an hour afterwards, the wind shifting to the west and blowing with tremendous force, a mountainous sea getting up drove us back into the South Atlantic.

The moment the wind abated we again made sail, and endeavoured to regain our lost ground. It was trying work. The weather was bitterly cold—the days little more than seven hours long—we scarcely ever had a dry rag on our backs, for when the rain was not falling the sea was continually breaking over us, knocking away our bulwarks, and threatening to carry off those on deck to destruction. Scarcely had we made good forty or fifty miles to the westward, than the wind increasing we had again to heave to under a close-reefed fore-topsail. Here we lay day after day, drifting rapidly back from the point it had taken us so long to gain. Each day, too, saw our bulwarks more and more shattered by the furious seas constantly breaking on board.

During this time I was one forenoon in the pantry, just outside the captain's cabin, when Domingo, handing me a wooden bowl containing the ingredients for a plum pudding, said, " Here you, Jack, carry dis to de galley, and tell de cook to boil him well."

I was bound to obey the steward, black though he was, and away I sped on my errand. Just as I reached the deck the ship gave a lurch and sent me down to leeward, when instead of, as I ought to have done, making my way up to windward, to save the distance, I ran along on the lee side of the deck. Before, however, my destination was reached I saw rising up right ahead a high, dark, foam-crested sea. On it came. With a crash like thunder it broke on board, and rushed roaring and hissing along the deck. Letting go the bowl, I frantically clutched a handspike sticking in the windlass, the nearest object to me. The fierce water surrounded me, the handspike unshipped, and, still grasping it, I felt myself borne away into the seething, hissing ocean. At that instant the ship gave another lee-lurch—all hope was gone—every incident of my life passed through my mind—when I caught a glimpse of the cook darting out of his galley; seizing me by the collar he dragged me in, dripping wet and half stunned. It was the work of a moment.

Directly afterwards the watch on the quarter-deck came hurrying forward with the third mate, who sang out, in a tone of alarm, "Where is that boy?" making sure that I had been carried overboard, he not having seen the cook lift me into the galley. When he found me there—though I fancied that I deserved commiseration, for my teeth chattered with cold and fright, and I looked like a drowned rat—he rated me soundly for having gone along the lee side. Medley, however, who had come with the rest, took me down below and made me shift into a dry suit of his clothing. He then persuaded Domingo to mix a fresh pudding, which he took to the cook to boil, so that I was saved from the captain's anger, which would have fallen on my head had it not been forthcoming at dinner-time.

On his return to the half-deck, Medley said to me, " Now, Jack, let us thank our merciful Father in heaven that you have been preserved from the greatest danger you were ever in during your life. Had the cook not been looking your way in another moment of time you would have been overboard, and it would have been impossible to pick you up."

I was willing to do as he proposed, and no one being below we knelt down by the side of our bunks, and I prayed more earnestly than I had ever prayed before. We were just about to rise from our knees when I heard Dan Hogan's voice exclaim, " Arrah now, you young psalm singers, what new trick are you after ? "

" Not a new trick, but an old custom, Dan," answered Medley, boldly confronting him. " If your life had just been saved I hope that you would thank God for it, otherwise I should say that you were a very ungrateful fellow."

" I 'm shut up," answered Hogan, and taking the article he had come for he returned on deck.

I expected that he would tell the men how he had found us employed, but I could not discover that he had spoken about it to any one, and after that he appeared to treat Medley with more respect than heretofore. When a person is doing a right thing the proper way is to confront his opponent boldly.

All this time we were suffering from the bitter cold, the sleet and snow, the long, long hours of darkness with seldom a gleam from the sun during the short period he was above the horizon. At length, the weather moderating, we again stood on our course to the westward.

About five weeks after we first sighted the Horn we managed to weather it, and finally steering northward with a favourable breeze soon ran into a more temperate atmosphere than we had enjoyed for many a day.

CHAPTER III.

E were now fairly in the Pacific. I have said little about our crew· There were some good men, not a few indifferent ones, and others as bad as could be. Dan Hogan was not by a long way the worst. It required the greatest strictness and vigilance on the part of the officers to keep them in order. Medley and I kept pretty clear of them, except when on duty, and we were then compelled to lend a hand to any one of them who might summon us. This we did cheerfully, though I, being the youngest, had all sorts of odd jobs to perform, not all of the pleasantest description. I thus had opportunities of hearing what the men were talking about without intending to be an eavesdropper, and I was before long convinced that some of them, if they had the opportunity, would not scruple to mutiny, to knock all who opposed them on the head, and take possession of the ship, or to run off themselves. I told Medley of my suspicions.

"It's all brag, Jack," he answered. "Don't trouble yourself about the matter. They might very probably like to do that, or any other piece of villany, but they dare not. They are cowards at heart, let them talk ever so boastfully."

I was not convinced, and determined to watch them. While we were engaged in the chase of whales, in towing them alongside, and in cutting out and trying in, or, in other words, in taking off the blubber and boiling it down into oil, they were too actively employed to plot mischief. They were also then separated, some being in the boats and others on board; but while the ship was at anchor off some savage island, away from all constituted authority, was the time when they were likely to carry out their evil designs.

I am sorry to say it, that though Captain Hake was a bold seaman, generous and kind-hearted, he was influenced by no religious principle; he objected to what he called Methodism on board, and so did the mate and doctor. Not a chest except Medley's and mine contained a Bible, and we had to read ours in secret to avoid the risk of being ordered to throw them overboard. If we had had merely to endure the sneers and laughter of our shipmates, we should not have minded. How I should have acted if left to myself, or with a different sort of companion, I do not know; but he encouraged me to read and pray, and refrain from evil habits, for which I owe him a deep debt of gratitude.

The first land we made was Juan Fernandez, or, as we called it, Robinson Crusoe's Island, where he, or rather Alexander Selkirk, lived so long till rescued by the ship in which the veteran Dampier sailed as pilot. It is about three hundred miles west of Valparaiso, on the coast of Chili, very mountainous and rugged, but richly covered with vegetation. We hove to off the bay in which Drake, Cavendish, Dampier, and Lord Anson anchored. Three boats were immediately sent on shore. I went in one with the doctor, who wanted to collect a species of mint, an excellent preventive against scurvy. It was found in such abundance that two boats loaded with it were sent back to the ship. We made tea of it, which we much enjoyed, after having had only pea-coffee to drink for so long. I half expected to meet Robinson Crusoe himself coming down to welcome us to his island, for we saw numbers of his goats among the craigs, though we in vain tried to catch one of the patriarchs of the flock, to ascertain whether its ears were nicked. Anson's men discovered several venerable animals with long beards, which had evidently been so treated by Selkirk himself, but that generation must have long since died out. The dogs Anson saw have also disappeared, being more easily shot than the goats.

Pulling a short distance from the shore, we got out our fishing-lines. So beautifully clear was the water as the sun shone down into it, that we could actually see the fish take the hook. They bit with wonderful avidity, and in a short time we caught as many rock-cod and other fish as we required. After this we stood along the coast, seldom within sixty miles of it, yet in sight of the snowy summits of the towering Andes. This part of the ocean is called by whalers "the off-shore fishing ground," extending from Valparaiso to Panama, and about four hundred miles westward from the land. We were tolerably successful, having killed four whales.

I shall not forget the scene the deck presented to my eyes the night after the blubber from our first whale had been stripped off and cut up while the crew were engaged in "trying out," that is, boiling it down into oil, to be stowed away in casks below. Along the deck were arranged the huge "try-pots," with brightly blazing fires beneath them, the fuel being the crisp membrane from the already used blubber.

On each side of the "try-works" were copper tanks or coolers to receive the oil as it flows over the sides of the pots with the rolling of the ship, or is ladled into them when sufficiently boiled. Some of the men stripped to the waist, and, begrimed with smoke and oil, were working away with forks or ladles, either throwing in the blubber, chopped into small pieces, or skimming off the scraps, or baling out the oil; others of the men were in the blubber-room, heaving on deck the horse-pieces, of about thirty pounds weight each, to be minced fine before being thrown into the try-pots. The whole watch were thus engaged, and what with the blazing fires, the wreaths of black smoke, the dark figures flourishing their implements, and ever and anon giving vent to horrible oaths and shouts and shrieks of savage laughter, the spectacle I beheld was more weird and wild than anything I could have imagined—like one of those dreadful scenes I have read of where spirits of darkness are described holding their midnight revels.

My share of the work on such occasions when the watch to which I belonged was on deck was to turn the grindstone for the carpenter, whose business it was to sharpen the spades for the men. In the intervals during daylight I amused myself, armed with one of the spades, the pole of which was twenty feet long, in killing the sharks swarming alongside. One deep cut on the back of the neck or tail was sufficient to destroy the largest of the savage creatures. I must not be accused of cruelty to animals. Of all the fierce creatures of land or sea the sailor most dreads and detests the cruel shark, for there are few who have not heard or seen some thing of his depredations.

About a month after leaving Juan Fernandez we reached the Galapagos, a group of volcanic islands lying under the equator, their black and rugged shores having a most uninviting appearance. In one only, Charles Island, is water to be found, though in another of considerable extent there are hills and valleys with groves of trees; but the chief vegetation on all of them is the prickly pear, which in most parts covers the ground.

We cruised off the Galapagos for upwards of two months, sometimes in company with other whalers, but more frequently alone, meeting with fair success. At last many of the men began to grumble at being kept so long at sea; those especially who had before shown a mutinous disposition taking no pains to conceal their discontent, for we had been ten

. months from the Thames, and according to the articles we were bound to anchor in a civilised port at least once in every six months. I felt sure from what I overheard that mischief was brewing; and one day when Domingo, whom I could not trust, was out of the cabin, I told the captain my fears. He only replied by a scornful laugh, but before he went on deck he put a brace of pistols in his belt, and I observed shortly afterwards that the mates had also armed themselves, while the muskets, cutlasses, tomahawks, and boarding-pikes were placed in a side cabin kept locked. The captain, however, knowing that the men had the right to put into port, informed them, after we had finished stowing the oil from the last whale caught, that he was about to steer for the coast of South America.

In about a week we made the land near the Gulf of Guayaquil, and thence ran down to Tumbez, an open roadstead, in which we brought up about a mile from the mouth of a river with a bar across it. Here the crew, instead of enjoying the rest they expected, were employed in towing off rafts of wood and water through the heavy surf setting on the shore. It was very hard work under a blazing sun, but still necessary, and the true men did not complain, though the others did pretty loudly, notwithstanding that few captains were more considerate in not over-working their crews than was ours. I heard him tell the first mate that as soon as the task was performed he intended to let them all go on shore, a watch at a time, to amuse themselves.

The first day's work was over, the boats hoisted up, and the anchor watch set, when I turned into my bunk. It seemed but a moment afterwards that Medley called me to keep the middle watch. I had just got on deck and was looking aft when I saw four figures lowering, as it seemed to me, the starboard quarter boat. Suspecting that something was wrong I looked round for the officer of the watch, but could no-where see him. He must, I guessed, have gone below. I was about to hurry into the cabin, but before I could make many steps aft I was seized, gagged, and dragged forward, where I was lashed to the windlass. I could just make out through the gloom that the boat was no longer in her place, and presently I saw several figures carry-ing some bags go forward and disappear from the spritsail yard. I knew, therefore, that the men I had seen intended to run away, and that they were probably some of the fellows whose complaints I had overheard. In vain I struggled to get free that I might give the alarm. These very men must have formed the watch, for no one came near me.

Daylight came at last, and the morning watch appearing on deck, I was released and taken to the captain, to whom I gave an account of what I had seen. Two boats were instantly sent in chase of the fugitives, who were the armourer, two boat-steerers, and three seamen. After some time the boats returned unsuccessful. The captain took the matter very quietly : "A good riddance, more thorough scoundrels I never had under me," he observed. To show his confidence in the rest he allowed the whole crew to go on shore, first one watch and then the other, for three days each, but as most of them were drunk all the time they would have been better on board. Sailing for the Marquesas, instead of the runaways we shipped six Kanakas, or natives, an Englishman, a beachcomber, or runaway sailor, who had been living on the island for several years, a Portuguese, and a Sandwich Islander. I mention them to show the heterogeneous materials of which the crews of English whalers were composed.

Touching at Dominica we sailed for Samoa, where we remained for some time, and thence proceeded off the Kingsmill group, and from this to the Japan whaling ground. While on this station we got so damaged in a typhoon that we had to make the best of our way to Honolulu, in the Sandwich Islands, to refit. This accomplished we returned to the Marquesas to land the natives we took from thence, having obtained as many hands as we required at Honolulu. Another season having come round, we again cruised for nearly two months in the neighbourhood of the Galapagos. By this time Medley, having been long out of his apprenticeship, was rated as an able seaman, and young as I was I could do the duty of one as well as any of the old hands, and better than those we had shipped to supply the places of the deserters and mutineers; besides which I had as good a knowledge of navigation as any of the mates. I had no longer to turn the grindstone or to sweep out the cabin, those and similar duties being performed by a young Sandwich Islander, but still the captain declined to give me up my indentures, or rather to have my name placed on the articles as an able seaman. Of course I could not demand what I asked, so I had to submit; indeed the captain probably thought me unreasonable.

Calm as is in general this part of the Pacific, there are occasionally storms of terrific violence. We experienced one when cruising some way to the southward of the Galapagos, but as we had plenty of sea room and were prepared for it we escaped without material damage. Two days afterwards, while the boats were away in chase of a whale, and I was aloft looking out for the appearance of others, I sighted a sail to the south-west standing towards us. I announced the fact by the usual cry of "Sail ho!" but as we had to follow our boats we could not go to meet her. As she drew nearer, I observed that her fore-topmast, her main-topgallantmast, and main-topsail yard were gone, and that she was evidently in other ways much damaged. The stranger passing within hail, a voice inquired, "What ship is that?" the third mate, Mr. Reece, answered, and put the usual questions in return, but before these could be replied to, gliding by she had rounded to a short distance off. As I watched her I saw two females, who had apparently just come on deck to look at us. Presently a boat was lowered which soon came alongside, when who, to my surprise, should step on board but my old friend Captain Bland. I at once concluded that the two females I had seen were Mary and her mother, and my heart gave a bound at the thoughts of meeting them. Our visitor first inquired for Captain Hake, and hearing that he was away in one of the boats his eye ranged along the deck as if in search of somebody. Though I was near him he did not recognise me till I advanced, when his eye brightened, and putting out his hand he shook mine cordially.

"Mrs. Bland and Mary will be right glad to see you, Jack, and to give you all the news from home, and you must try to cheer them up by telling them all you have been about, for they have had a trying time of it for some months past. As soon as Captain Hake returns I will get him to allow you to accompany me on board the 'Lady Alice.'" He then addressed Mr. Reece: "Your ship and mine belong to the same owners, and I want as many of your men as can be spared to assist my people in repairing our damages, for we are terribly short-handed. We encountered fearful weather in coming round Cape Horn, when we had the misfortune to lose four men overboard, three more were killed by the only whale we have yet taken, two deserted at Juan Fernandez with the idea of playing Robinson Crusoe, though they'll very soon get sick of that, and five others are too sick to come on deck. Three days ago we were caught in a gale, and before the hands could shorten sail the topmasts were carried over the side, so you'll understand that we want all the help we can get."

"I've no doubt that the captain will afford it, sir," answered Mr. Reece; "but we ourselves are sadly wanting in able seamen—we haven't more than three hands who can be trusted to take the helm with any sea on."

Medley and I smiled at the mate's remark, for we believed that we could steer as well as he could, and that there were several others who could do so. A shout from the look-out aloft announced that a whale was killed, and we bore down to meet the boats towing it towards us. The captured whale was nearly eighty feet long, and worth a thousand pounds at least. Our captain was, therefore, in very good humour, and cordially greeted Captain Bland, promising to do all he could to help him, but, of course, till the oil from the whale alongside was stowed away he could spare no hands.

"But you will let my young friend, Jack Kemp, and your other apprentice, Medley, go with me?" said Captain Bland. "They can best be spared at present, and I can trust them to assist my mates in superintending the work."

The captain demurred to this, as I was especially useful to him. I used to work all his observations, make out his bills for the men, keep the slop-locker in order, serve out the stores, and besides many other duties, act as his barber. My kind friend, however, pressed the point, and at length the captain consented to let us go, accompanied by two of the Kroomen, promising shortly to follow the "Lady Alice" to Charles' Island, one of the Galapagos.

Medley and I were not long in cleaning ourselves and putting on our Sunday best, and with our working clothes in our bags we stepped into Captain Bland's boat. By this time the two vessels were some way apart, so that we had a long pull. As we got near the "Lady Alice" I saw Mrs. Bland and Mary looking over the side, but they made no signal of recognition, so that it was evident they did not know me; they did not do so even when I stepped on deck. Perhaps I might not have known Mary, for she had grown from a little girl into almost a young woman, and very bright and pleasant she looked, which is better to my mind than what some people call beautiful. I saw her eyes as they turned towards me brighten, while a smile rose on her lips.

"What! haven't you brought Jack Kemp with you?" asked Mrs. Bland of her husband.

"Yes, there he is; I knew him," cried Mary, springing forward and taking my hand.

Mrs. Bland embraced me, as if she were my mother. "I told her I would, Jack," she said.

" She often felt very anxious about you for fear you should get into the rough ways of your ship-mates, and be no longer what you once were, a good, affectionate lad. You are not changed, Jack, I hope, though you have grown so big and manly."

I could nearly have cried, I felt so happy, as I answered, " I hope not, Mrs. Bland, and I have to thank my friend Medley here for assisting me to act rightly."

" A Christian friend is a valuable help on board ship, as well as everywhere else," observed Captain Bland. " I am truly glad that you have found such an one in Andrew Medley, whose father I have the pleasure of knowing. It will do his heart good to hear this account of his son. I wish there were more like you two young men at sea."

The ladies now invited us into the cabin to have some tea, and as we sat there, helped by Mary, we felt quite like different beings to those we had been for so many months past.

I heard some of the news from home, which I need not repeat, but we had not much time for conversation, as, having shifted into our working clothes, we had to hurry on deck to assist the crew in getting the ship to rights. We and our two Kroomen set to with a will, and three of the sick men turned out of their bunks to help. It was heavy work though, and in addition during two hours in each watch we had to keep the pumps going. While daylight lasted Mary remained on deck, and her presence incited us to exertion. I thought of the danger to which she would be exposed should bad weather again come on, and the ship not be prepared to encounter it.

At length we entered the harbour, a gloomy enough looking place, surrounded by high, black, rugged cliffs, yet being well protected from all winds, we were glad to find ourselves safe in it. I almost dreaded the arrival of the "Eagle," as I feared that I should have to return to her and my rough associates. It was not the hard work I disliked, but the utter want of humanising influences on board the "Eagle," whereas, independent of the effect produced by Mrs. Bland and Mary, a far higher moral tone prevailed on board the "Lady Alice"; the mates were well-conducted men, and several among the crew were real Christians, who made the Bible the rule of life. I do not mean to say that the ship was a perfect Paradise; there were some bad, wild characters, but they were kept in check by the rest. We were too busy to escort the ladies on shore, and they had no fancy to go by themselves, although there were neither wild beasts nor savages to be feared. We were waiting, however, for the arrival of the "Eagle" to heave the ship down, so as to get at the leak; and as the position she would then be in would make the cabin a very uncomfortable habitation, Captain Bland proposed rigging a tent on the beach under the cliffs in which his wife and daughter might live till the work was accomplished.

As soon, therefore, as Medley and I with two of the men could be spared, we accompanied the captain on shore, taking with us some spars, rope, sails, and spare canvas. It was evident that the spot the captain first thought of would be too hot, as not a breath of air reached it, so he selected another further from the ship in a more open situation. Here, having beaten smooth the black lava-like soil, we soon had up a good-sized tent with three compartments—one for the captain and Mrs. Bland, one for Mary, and a third for a sitting-room. This done, while the boat returned for some furniture and cooking utensils, the captain sent me to the top of a cliff overlooking the ocean to the southward to ascertain if the "Eagle" was in sight. I had not been long looking out when I saw a sail standing for the island, but after watching her for some time I was convinced that she was not the "Eagle," but a much smaller craft. As she drew still nearer I perceived, indeed, that she was a schooner, apparently a Spanish vessel, though she showed no flag. Instead, however, of steering for the harbour where the "Lady Alice" lay, she kept round the island to another on the other side. What she was, or why she had come to the island, I could not conjecture. I was about to return when I caught sight of a speck of white canvas above the horizon. "That probably is the 'Eagle,'" I thought. "In a few days I shall have to bid my kind friends farewell and go back to my duties on board her."

As there was a fine breeze the ship rapidly approached, and as I had no doubt that she was the "Eagle," I went back to the tent to tell Captain Bland that she was in sight, as also to describe to him the schooner I had seen.

"She has probably come across from Payta to catch turtle or fish," he observed. "We are not likely to see any of her crew, unless they think that they can get a good price from us for what they bring."

We now returned on board to describe to the ladies the preparations we had made for them. Captain Bland then had all the boats manned to assist in towing in the "Eagle" should the wind fall light, as it frequently did towards evening. At length Medley, who had landed and gone to the top of the cliff, made the signal that she was near, on which all the boats, with flags flying in the bows, pulled out of the harbour. We saw her about two miles off already nearly becalmed. As we got near her crew greeted us with a cheer, and without stopping to ask questions we took hold of the tow ropes, when, giving way with a will, joined by her boats already lowered, we made the big ship glide through the water at the rate of nearly three miles an hour. We thus soon brought the ship to an anchor in the harbour, when Captain Hake came on board the " Lady Alice," and undertook to do all his brother captain required. He was in high good humour at having captured another whale, which had caused the " Eagle " to be so much longer in making her appearance than we expected. I thought that now would be the time to get Captain Bland to beg him to allow me to remain on board the " Lady Alice." The same idea occurred to Mary, who I saw whispering to her father. Captain Bland kindly pressed the point.

"What am I to do without my barber and clerk and storekeeper, I should like to know ?" exclaimed Captain Hake. " Why the young fellow works all my observations for me. No, no. Be reasonable, Bland; he is bound to me remember. I will lend him to you now, but when the 'Eagle' leaves this harbour he goes in her."

I thought that it was my captain who was not reasonable. I felt dreadfully disappointed, but I was his slave, and compelled to submit.

CHAPTER IV.

APTAIN HAKE invited Mrs. Bland and Mary to take up their abode on board the " Eagle " while the Lady Alice was hove down, and looked much disappointed when he heard that a tent had been put up for them on shore. I need not describe the operation of heaving down further than by saying that the topmasts being struck, the cargo landed, and the ballast shifted, the ship is heeled over on one side, till her keel can be seen, then stages are slung, so that every part may be easily reached. When one side is repaired she is turned over, and the other is treated in the same way.

Before commencing operations Medley and I were engaged for some hours in securing all the things in the cabins, so that nothing might be broken, while the bedding and many other articles were carried on shore. I suggested to Captain Bland that it would be prudent to have a guard near him at night, and begged that he would allow Medley and me, with our faithful Kroomen, Pepper and Salt, and four of his own most trustworthy men, to put up a couple of rough tents, which would afford sufficient shelter to us in that warm climate.

"Do as you like, Jack," he answered. "We shall be glad of your company in the evening, but I do not apprehend the slightest risk by our remaining on shore alone."

I carried out my proposal, each of us having a musket and ammunition, and a very pleasant evening Medley and I spent in the tent, Captain Hake not making his appearance, as we feared he would. Of course we went off at daybreak to the ship, as we had to work as hard as the rest. Having knocked off, however, an hour or so before nightfall, we hurried on shore, when Mary asked us to escort her on an exploring trip into the island.

"I should like to climb to the top of yonder high hill," she said; "we may get there and back before dark, I am sure."

"If you don't mind our being in our working suits, Miss Bland," observed Medley. "It would take us some time to polish up."

"I quite forgot how you were dressed," she answered, laughing; "I only knew that you had been engaged in a necessary duty, which has, now I come to look at you, certainly made you unusually tarry and grimy. However, we are not likely to meet anybody else who will mind how you look, so pray let us set off."

We started, Medley and I carrying our muskets, in case we should meet with any strange creature we might wish to shoot—though we knew that there were no alligators or pumas, or other savage beasts such as are found on the neighbouring continent. The scenery was certainly not picturesque. Out of the black tufa-formed soil on the lower ground grew numerous curiously-shaped cacti, or prickly pear shrubs, and we caught sight in the distance of one or two monster terrapins crawling among them. At last we reached the entrance of a narrow valley, in which, to our surprise, we found a luxuriant tropical vegetation, not only of grass and shrubs, but of trees of considerable height, produced, we had no doubt, by a fountain of clear water which, issuing from the mountain's side at the farther end, flowed down the centre in a babbling stream of some width, though what afterwards became of it we could not discover. Numberless birds, several of gay plumage, flew about in all directions, and were so tame that they perched on the branches close to us whenever we stopped, as if to ask

what we wanted in their domain, and three
at different times settled on Mary's head or
shoulders.

Medley was going to shoot at some which
looked like pigeons, but she cried out, "For
shame! I would not for the world have the beautiful things killed. They trust us, and it would be
a cruel return for their confidence."

My messmate immediately lowered his gun.
"You are right, Miss Bland," he answered; "I did
not consider what I was about to do."

He shortly afterwards proposed climbing to
the top of a cliff from which he expected to obtain
a view over the island to the northward. As this
was a task Mary was unable to accomplish, I
remained with her while he set off alone. As I
saw by the sun that it was high time to commence
our return, I told him that we would walk on
slowly towards the tents, so that he might overtake us. I cannot say that I was exactly in a hurry
for him to do so, as Mary and I being old friends
we naturally had a good deal to talk about which
could not interest him. At last, however, it
struck me that he ought to have caught us up;
on looking back I saw him running towards us.
On our stopping to allow him to come up he
made a sign to us to go on. Had I been alone
I should have waited, but though I could not

divine what danger threatened I thought it prudent to hurry Mary on.

"What can he have seen to alarm him?" she asked.

"That is more than I can say, but he is not a person to be alarmed without reason," I answered.

"It is said that these islands were produced by volcanoes; perhaps one has just burst forth, and he fears that the lava may overtake us."

"We should have heard the noise and seen the fire and smoke if that were the case," I replied.

"Then it is possible that he may have seen some wild beast which was not known to exist here," she observed. "Do you think so?"

Medley, who at that moment overtook us, answered the question, "Not a wild beast, Miss Bland, but a set of ruffians, whom it might be dangerous for you to meet; I saw them just below me carousing round a blazing fire, at which they had been cooking a terrapin, or some other animal. As I crept nearer to find out who they were, I at once guessed their character by their horrible oaths, the snatches of ribald songs and savage laughter which reached my ears. I got near enough even to distinguish the features of several of them, among whom I recognised Tom Moon, the armourer, and Jos Mortis, both of whom were among the rascals who ran off with our whale boat from Tumbez, you remember, Jack. I think there were others of the gang, but would not be certain. I was retiring when Moon caught sight of me and shouted to his companions to give chase. Fortunately most of them were too drunk to make much headway, but seeing that some of them were coming, I judged it prudent to run on and warn you, for I suspect that they are ready for any kind of atrocity."

While my messmate was giving this account we were hurrying on—indeed there was no time to lose under any circumstances, for almost directly after the sun had set it would become dark, and we might have much difficulty in finding our way. I frequently looked back with some anxiety, and fancied that I saw several men in the distance, but we still hoped to reach the tents before they could come up with us. Medley and I were resolved, should they do so, to keep them at bay with our muskets till Mary had effected her escape. She kept up her spirits, not being as much alarmed as I thought she would have been. I was greatly relieved when at length we saw the white tops of the tents. As we got nearer I shouted, and soon Captain Bland appeared, followed by Pepper and Salt.

"You have been too long away, young people,

E

and I was on the point of setting out to look for you; however, as I have no doubt that you have plenty of good excuses to offer, you are forgiven," he said, in his kind, cheery way. When Medley told him of the sort of characters we had seen he expressed his satisfaction that we had avoided them. "They probably belong to the schooner you saw standing in for the island the other day, Jack; and if so, the chances are that she is not the honest fisherman we supposed," he remarked. "We must keep a watch on the fellows in case they should come this way."

Though he said this he did not appear to be much troubled about the matter, and we were soon all seated at Mrs. Bland's tea-table in her tent. I, however, had told Pepper and Salt, whom I could trust, to be on the look-out, so that we might not be taken by surprise. We spent the evening happily as usual, Mary singing to her guitar, while the kind captain told some of his best stories, at which he always laughed most heartily himself. I made an excuse two or three times to go out, to be sure that the Kroomen were on the alert, and I also visited the seamen's tent, and told them to be ready to turn out if necessary.

"All right, Jack," said the captain, guessing what I had been about. "You've got the wise prudence of a careful officer in you, though I don't think the roistering crew Medley saw will attempt to make their way to-night thus far from their camp."

When I again sat down the captain told the last of his stories for the night, and Mary sang another song; but scarcely had her sweet notes died away than Pepper's rough voice was heard shouting, "Who go dere! Stop or shoot!"

"Who says that?" exclaimed an English voice, though as gruff as the black's.

"I say dat," cried Salt, who was at some distance from his companion. "Take care—I see you."

I guessed that the Kroomen, favoured by the colour of their skins, had concealed themselves, so that the intruders were puzzled as to their whereabouts, and afraid to approach. Medley and I hurried out of the tent, and calling up the seamen, who followed us with their muskets, went to where the Kroomen were posted. The ground rising slightly, we could see several dark figures in front of us against the sky moving about, but I doubted whether they could make us out. If the pirates, for such we had good reason to suppose they were, had expected to take us by surprise they were disappointed. Our men cocked their muskets with loud clicks, which might easily have been heard by them. We waited in silence to see what they would do, but they seemed undecided. Presently we were joined by Captain Bland.

"What is it you want here, my men?" he shouted. "We can receive no visitors to-night. To-morrow morning if you come back we will hear what you have to say."

The pirates must have guessed who spoke to them, for one of them immediately answered, "Just listen, captain; we want some bread and rum, and salted pork, and a supply of powder and lead, with some shot, and a few other things. We wish to be moderate, but the things we must have to-morrow morning as soon as you can send on board for them if you haven't brought enough on shore."

"As to that I can make no promise, so good-night to you, men," said the captain, in a firm tone.

The strangers made no reply, but we could hear them talking among themselves. Presently one of them shouted, "We must take what we want!" and the whole gang, numbering three times as many as our party, uttering savage shouts, came rushing on, till, when they were within twenty yards of us, the Kroomen, without waiting for orders, fired at them. They, on this, hesitated for a moment, and then there came a random volley from muskets and pistols, the shots whistling past our ears. A dreadful idea occurred to me.

"Mrs. Bland and Mary may be hurt, sir," I exclaimed.

"No fear of that, my lad," said the captain; "I bade them lie down under their bedding, for I thought that the rascals might use their fire-arms."

Just as he spoke the pirates began again to advance, though with more caution than at first, but they had not moved many steps when the four seamen fired, and the Kroomen, who had quickly reloaded, did the same. This again checked the advance of the pirates, who probably did not expect to meet with so warm a reception.

"Reserve your fire the rest of you," shouted the captain, to give the fellows the idea that we had more men ready to receive them should they venture to come on. Strange to say, none of our party were hit, nor, as far as we could tell, were any of them brought to the ground. Providentially for us, the whole of the pirates being drunk, and many of them cowards at heart, instead of rushing forward, as we had expected them to do, they retired to a distance, shouting and swearing at us as they went off. I thought that Captain Bland would now send his wife and daughter out of danger on board the "Eagle," but he considered that by so doing the few men who remained might be overpowered, and his property left to the mercy of the pirates.

"I don't think that the fellows will return, and if they do we must treat them as before," he observed. "The chances are that in a short time they will be all fast asleep. They attacked us in a drunken freak more than with any settled plan."

For some time it appeared that he was right. He returned to the tent to relieve the anxiety of his wife and daughter, while Medley and I mounted guard with Pepper and Salt, telling the other men that we expected them to relieve us in a couple of hours. Before half that time, however, had expired, we heard the pirates again coming on. Presently, giving vent to the most fearful shouts and shrieks, they fired a volley at us and then came rushing on. Their voices aroused our companions, who sprang out to our assistance, while Captain Bland, who had been on the alert, also joined us.

"Kneel down, lads, and do not fire till I give the word," he said, in a low voice.

We obeyed him, and scarcely had we done so

than the pirates, still shouting and shrieking, discharged their pieces, the shot, however, flying over our heads; then on they again came, but before they got much nearer, a hearty cheer rose from the direction of the beach, and some thirty men or more from the two ships, armed with pikes, cutlasses, and muskets, came tramping up, again cheering lustily. We all fired just before they joined us. The pirates did not stop to encounter them, but scampered off as fast as their legs could carry them, several throwing down their weapons the more quickly to escape. Captain Hake, who led the party just landed, followed with most of the men for some distance, but no one could move rapidly over the rough ground, and the pirates, favoured by the darkness, and better acquainted with the country than we were, effected their escape. Though there was very little chance of their again molesting us, watch was kept during the night. Captain Hake said that on hearing the firing, suspecting that we were attacked, though by whom he could not conjecture, he had lowered his own boats, and summoned Captain Bland's crew to our assistance. The next morning a party set off to try and capture our assailants, but they had managed to reach their schooner, which was seen standing out to sea. Though no dead bodies were found, marks of blood seen on the rocks showed that several had been wounded.

Mary was unwilling to make any more distant excursions, but she and her mother continued to reside on the island till the " Lady Alice " was ready for sea. Now came the moment of trial. Captain Hake had been specially civil whenever he met me in company with Captain Bland, and I began to hope that he would allow me to join the " Lady Alice." My old friend at length once more pressed the point. Captain Hake at once assumed the stern manner he knew well how to put on.

" I mustn't let the lad think too much of himself ; but it 's just this, Captain Bland, you want him and so do I, and as I have a right to him I intend to keep him. He rejoins the ' Eagle ' this evening."

Captain Bland could not complain. He had received great assistance from Captain Hake, who lent him Pepper and Salt and two Sandwich islanders, with which addition to his crew, now that the rest were well, he was able to continue his fishing. Mary, however, was very indignant with Captain Hake, and went so far as to call him a hard-hearted, cruel man, who wanted me to do all his drudgery, instead of allowing me to act as an officer with her father.

The next morning we sailed, and for some time kept company. I was glad to see the "Lady Alice" shortly afterwards take two whales, for I felt as much interest in her success as in that of our own ship. Twice we were becalmed when close together, and Medley and I got leave to pay a visit to our friends. I need not say that we were most kindly received. It seemed to us like going out of the rough world into a small paradise when we entered the pretty neat cabin, and were seated at the table with Mary and good Mrs. Bland. Medley had a talent for drawing, and used to make pictures of ships and scenes descriptive of whale-catching for Mary, which we thought very good and true to nature. Among them were two—one of a ship leaving port, another of one returning.

"I wish this was the 'Lady Alice,'" said Mary, taking up the last. "It will be truly a happy day when we get back with dear father safe."

"I hoped that you were enjoying your cruise, and would be in no hurry to have it over," I observed.

"So I do on many accounts," she answered. "But I am always anxious when I see father go out to attack a huge whale. Two of our men were killed by one, and father might share the same fate. Sometimes his boat is a long, long way out of sight of the ship, and we cannot tell what is happening."

"You must just trust in God, Miss Bland," observed Medley. "He is doing his duty, and you can pray that he may be protected."

"I always try to do that; but still, you know, the danger is great, and that makes me wish to be safe at home again, though I fear that you will be there so long before us that you will have sailed again to some distant part of the world perhaps, and we may never see you more."

"Perhaps the 'Lady Alice' will be more fortunate than you expect, and may soon get filled up," I answered, wishing to restore her spirits, which, for some reason, were unusually low. Was it on account of some unseen danger threatening us?

For several weeks we continued in company, both ships being tolerably successful; but the "Lady Alice" certainly killed more whales than we did, simply, I believe, because a better lookout was kept. Yet Captain Bland never sent the boats away on a Sunday, while all days were alike to Captain Hake. I judged by his remarks that he was somewhat jealous of the better fortune of his brother commander. At last we lost sight of the "Lady Alice." Whenever I could manage it I went aloft to look out for her, but though I strained my eyes gazing round and round the horizon, I searched in vain. In what direction she had gone no one could say.

About a fortnight after this, when we were about fifty miles to the southward of the Galapagos, I one morning at sunrise having gone aloft, caught sight of a sail between us and the islands, and almost ahead. My heart gave a bound, for I made sure that she was the "Lady Alice." As, however, we neared her, when I again went aloft to look out, much to my disappointment I saw that she was a much smaller craft, a schooner, standing from the eastward for the islands. Another look at her a little later showed me that she was of the same size and appearance as that of the craft whose piratical crew had attacked us. I felt, indeed, convinced that she was the same. On coming down on deck I told the captain, unable, however, to conjecture what he would do. At first I thought it possible that he might make chase, and attempt to capture her; but then I reflected that though we had four guns she probably carried many more, with a larger crew, and that, at all events, we could not venture to fire at her unless she attacked us.

"We'll let her alone, Jack, whether she's the pirate. schooner or not, but we must take care that she does not come alongside the ship while the boats are away, or the rascals aboard her may take the liberty of relieving us of our money and stores," observed the captain.

The moment he said this the thought flashed across my mind, "What if she should have fallen in with the 'Lady Alice'?" The idea was too terrible to dwell on. Yet once conceived, I could not banish it from my mind. I spoke to Medley on the subject. He tried to console me by saying that even if the schooner we had seen was a pirate it was not at all likely that she should have fallen in with the "Lady Alice," and if she had, have ventured to attack her. As may be supposed, I more eagerly than ever looked out for our fellow-cruiser, but day after day went by and not a white speck denoting a distant sail was to be seen above the horizon.

We were all this time very unsuccessful in our business. We gave chase to three whales, which, one after the other, got away before the boats reached them. The captain swore that he would have the next. Not one was seen, however, for a whole week. The men grumbled and wondered why we remained on the station. At last one morning, just at daybreak, the look-out, who had just gone to the masthead, gave the welcome shout of " There she spouts! there she spouts!"

In a moment the watch on deck aroused those below by the loud stamping of their feet, and up they tumbled. The captain and mates rushed out from their cabins half-dressed. The four boats were lowered, and away they pulled in the direction the whale was seen, about two miles to windward. Medley and I, with two seamen, the doctor, and other idlers, remained to take care of the ship, and to beat her up after the boats. The whale sounded, and remaining down fifty minutes rose again nearer the ship, so that we could clearly see what took place.

The boats and their crews giving way with might and main, gathered round from different directions. The captain was the first to strike his harpoon into the whale, following the weapon with a couple of lances; he was fast, but he quickly backed off from the monster, which, leaping half out of the water, and turning partly round made a dash with open mouth at another boat coming up, and in an instant crushed it into fragments as if it had been built of paper. The crew sprang overboard on either side, endeavouring to escape—whether any were killed we could not ascertain—and the next instant the whale, raising its powerful flukes, struck a third boat, shattering her by the blow, and throwing her high into the air, bottom upwards, her people and gear being scattered around on the foam-covered surface of the water. The other boats pulled away to avoid the same fate, which it seemed likely would be theirs, for the old lone whale was savagely bent on mischief it was very evident, when he suddenly sounded, dragging out the line like lightning after him. A second line was secured to the first, but that reached the bitter end before the first mate's boat, engaged in trying to rescue the drowning men, could come up, and it was cut to save the boat from being dragged under water. Not till then could the captain go to the assistance of the people still struggling for their lives. Some were holding on to oars, others to fragments of planks. At length the survivors were picked up, and the two boats returned on board.

The men, as they came alongside, looked very downcast. Three of our shipmates had disappeared—two of whom had been crushed by the monster's jaws, the other killed by the blow of his flukes—as many more were severely injured, the third mate was among the killed. The captain, ordering the carpenter at once to put together two boats to supply the places of those destroyed, went to his cabin. I had never before seen him so much out of spirits. He seemed to think that some fatality was attending the voyage. In less than half an hour he returned on deck, looking flushed and excited.

"We must have that whale if we lose a couple more of our boats in taking him," he exclaimed, addressing the first mate. "Keep a bright look-out for him." This was not so easily done, for darkness was coming on, and the monster might possibly have swum away from the ship.

The mate answered, "Aye, aye, sir," and hailed the look-out aloft.

Some time passed and no whale appeared; a large one, such as that attacked, can remain down eighty minutes, and swim some distance in that time. At last night came down upon us, and the chances of discovering the creature decreased. The weather too, hitherto fine, changed, and before morning the ship was under close-reefed topsails, dashing through the fast-rising foaming seas. Had we got the whale alongside we should probably have had to cut from it. The captain, however, had no intention of giving up the search. We beat backwards and forwards in the neighbourhood for three days, till the gale abated, and then made several circuits round the spot, increasing the radius without seeing the old whale or any other.

The men who had before grumbled at being kept so long on the station now declared that the captain had gone out of his mind, and I feared that if he persisted much longer they would break into open mutiny. Still day after day he continued sailing round and round, till one morning when we had been running to the eastward, and he ordered the watch to brace up the yards, they stood with their hands in their pockets or folded on their breasts, while they stamped loudly with their feet. At that instant the watch below came rushing up on deck armed with weapons of all descriptions, some having muskets and pistols, others cutlasses, pikes, harpoons, and blubber spades. The captain on this, calling on the two mates, Medley, and me to stand by him, rushed into his cabin, from which he quickly returned with a rifle in his hand, and several pistols stuck in his belt. A shout of derisive laughter from the crew greeted him. He took no notice of it, but cried out to us, "Go and arm yourselves, and we 'll soon put down these mutinous rascals." As he spoke he raised his rifle, and half a dozen muskets were pointed at him. At that juncture the look-out at the masthead shouted, "A dead whale away to the southward!" "We must not lose it, sir," said the first mate. "Lads!" he cried, turning to the seamen, "we 'll settle this matter afterwards. Brace up the yards."

The men obeyed with alacrity, having stowed their weapons forward, while the captain placed his on the companion hatch. We were soon convinced that the object seen was a dead whale. Innumerable birds hovered above it, while the splashing in the water near it showed that also teemed with living creatures. The monster was worth a thousand pounds if we could secure its blubber, but as we got nearer the horrible odour which reached us even to windward put an end to our hopes. To have taken it alongside would have poisoned the whole crew. The captain, however, insisted on regaining his harpoon, and the ship being hove to he went away in a boat with a black crew. He did succeed in getting the harpoon, but the line was so completely coiled round and round the monster's body, into which it had cut deeply, that it could not be brought off. The captain looked very pale when he returned, and at once retired to his cabin. The blacks, though at first very sick from this horrible task, quickly recovered. The first mate, who had followed the captain below, soon coming again on deck told the men that he was ordered to shape a course for Tumbez, where the ship would remain for a fortnight, and all hands have leave to go on shore. A hearty cheer greeted this announcement, and the mutiny, which threatened not to end without bloodshed, was peaceably brought to a conclusion.

CHAPTER V.

THE recollection of the suspicious schooner was continually haunting me. Being unable also to account for our not having fallen in with the "Lady Alice" made me feel far from happy. Medley tried to cheer me up by suggesting that she had probably sailed for the westward, and that we should find her by-and-by in that direction. At last we reached the Bay of Tumbez, and came to an anchor off the mouth of the river. I looked eagerly out, half expecting to see the "Lady Alice" there, but no other English ship was in the roads besides ours. As soon as we had got off a supply of wood and water on rafts through the surf as before, the captain said, " Now, lads, I will fulfil my promise and allow you all a run on shore for three days, a watch at a time; I 'll pay for your lodging, but you must be back at the hour I fix."

The men expressed their satisfaction by a

cheer, and that they might have three full days, the starboard watch, to which I belonged, at once shoved off. A surf was breaking on the bar, where an upset would have been a serious matter, as sharks abounded ready to pick us up. We crossed, however, in safety, and pulled up the stream for five or six miles. The scenery was very pretty. In many places the trees grew thickly on the banks, their branches, among which numbers of amusing little monkeys were sporting, hanging completely over the water; now we could see the creatures peeping out at us from among the leaves; now they would skip off with wonderful activity; now come back and drop sticks and nuts down on our heads, keeping up a constant chattering all the time. As an American sailor observed, we might as well have tried to stop a flow of greased lightning as to lay hold of their tails.

While we were watching the monkeys I saw what I had taken to be a dead log begin slowly to move, and presently a huge pair of jaws opened and an alligator glided off the bank into deep water; we found, indeed, as we got higher up, that the river swarmed with alligators, so that none of us were disposed to take a bath in fresh water. We might have gone up to Tumbez by the river, but as this would have given us a long pull against the current, we landed at a plantation owned by a kind old lady, who offered us fruit and cakes and wine, and said that she should be happy to see me again.

We then proceeded for three miles or so through orange groves and sandhills to the town, a wretched tumble-down-looking place, half choked up with sand. Here, as it was now dark, we took shelter in a house called an inn, but, except in the public hall, where the eating and drinking went on, not a room contained a particle of furniture, so that we had to lie down on the floor and be devoured by mosquitoes and creeping things innumerable. There were several young Americans of a superior class with whom I had associated during the afternoon, and when we got up we agreed that the wisest thing we could do would be to get out of the town as fast as possible. We scarcely knew each other at first, so swollen were our faces and necks from the bites of the voracious insects. Early in the night the greater part of our men were drunk, and it appeared probable that before the day was much older the rest would be so. We, however, had to wait for breakfast, and before we left the whole place was in an uproar with tipsy seamen and natives quarrelling and fighting. Escaping from the disgraceful scene we made our way to the house of Donna Anna, the old lady who had been so civil to us when we landed. She received us very kindly, and hearing why we left the town commended us for our discretion, telling us that we were welcome to remain till we had to return to our ship. As the heat was too great to make us wish to go out, we spent the day lolling about in a cool room, and eating when food was brought to us. In the evening we strolled through the orange groves, eating as much of the fruit as we desired. Our hostess still further showed her kindness by supplying us with mosquito curtains to sleep under at night.

We were all sorry when the time came for us to embark, but our men did not make their appearance, and I don't know when they would have come had not the second mate gone into the town at daybreak and compelled the more sober to bring off the others. As we pulled down the river we met the captain coming up it to look for us. He was very angry, and declared that he was much inclined not to let the other watch go on shore on account of the behaviour of the men. He relented, however, charging them to look out how they conducted themselves.

Soon after they had shoved off, the first mate said that he saw a small craft of some sort under sail coming in from the offing. All the telescopes on board were at once directed towards her, and before long she was pronounced to be a whale boat. On she came, steering for our ship, which, as we had the British flag flying, was easily distinguished from the American's. The crew were lying along on the thwarts, the heads of two of them just raised above the gunwale, as if their eyes were directed towards us; one man only was sitting up steering, and he was leaning back seemingly in an exhausted state. I looked at him several times through my glass till the boat drew nearer, when I was convinced that he was **my** kind friend Captain Bland. Yes, there was no doubt about it. Fearful apprehensions crowded into my mind. What could have become of the " Lady Alice " ?—had any accident happened to her ? Captain Bland would, I was certain, not willingly have deserted his wife and daughter. How eager I felt to inquire !

Directly the boat came alongside the mate and I, with two other men, descended to assist up the people in her. " Take them first ; they want help more than I do," said the captain, pointing to the others, one of whom kept murmuring, " Water ! water ! "

The others scarcely spoke. Captain Bland himself looked bad enough—so haggard and thin. We soon had him and the rest on deck and their boat hoisted in, when their captain was carried into Captain Hake's cabin. After he had taken some weak spirits and water and some food, he was able to speak without difficulty.

"O sir, do tell me where are Mrs. Bland, and Mary, and the 'Lady Alice,'" I said, as I was taking away his plate.

"I wish, Jack, that I could answer the question," he answered. "They will be fearfully anxious about me, but I trust that they and the ship are safe enough. Just a fortnight ago, when off the Galapagos, we sighted three whales. I went in chase of one of them to the northward The other boats pulled after the rest. The whale I was following headed away from the ship, but still I hoped to come up with him before dark and make him my prize; I had nearly succeeded, and in another minute should have had my harpoon in his side, when he turned flukes and disappeared. Though the sun was setting, I expected that he would come up again while there was light enough to strike him, so waited on the look-out, but the weather changed; a thick mist came up, the night became very dark, and though we heard the sound of spouting in the distance during the night, when morning broke no whale was to be seen—nor was the ship in sight. Anxious to be on board, I steered in the direction where I expected to find her, with, as I hoped, one or two whales alongside. It was blowing fresh with some sea on, but not sufficient to make it necessary to cut the whale adrift, should one have been secured. Every hour I expected to come in sight of the ship, but we had reached the spot where I thought she would be found, and she was nowhere to be seen. We then steered to the southward and south-east, supposing that she might have stood after the boats in that direction. Once we saw a sail, some small craft, a schooner apparently; we tried to speak her, to learn if she had fallen in with the " Lady Alice," but she kept away from us. At length I came to the painful conclusion that if we did not before long fall in with the ship, we should run a fearful risk of being starved. We had providentially brought away a bag of biscuits of about fourteen pounds weight, half a dozen sausages, and a breaker of water, and we had besides a pound and a half of wax candles. A portion of the biscuits and sausages had already been consumed, but I now put the crew on an allowance, so that the food might last us for eight or nine days—the time I calculated it would take us, should the wind hold from the westward, to reach this place, for which I at once steered. The sausages were soon gone, and then the wax candles helped out the biscuits.

We should have died, I think, though, had not we caught six flying fish on one day and three another—for our last crumb of biscuit and drop of water were gone before we sighted the land."

"I hope that Captain Hake will at once sail in search of the 'Lady Alice,'" I exclaimed, "no time should be lost."

I thought of the schooner, but I did not mention my fears respecting her, lest I should increase the anxiety of my friend.

"Captain Hake has not yet offered to sail, but I trust that he will without delay," he answered.

Soon afterwards Captain Hake entered the cabin. My friend at once told him his wishes.

"Sorry that part of my crew are on shore; we must wait till they return," was his answer.

"Could not you send for them?" asked Captain Bland. "I wish to relieve the anxiety of my wife and daughter."

"I'll go on shore, sir, and bring them back!" I exclaimed, eagerly.

"More easily said than done," observed the captain. "However, you may go."

I hurried on deck, selected Pepper and Salt and two Sandwich islanders, all of whom I could trust—which I could not the English seamen—lowered a boat, and pulled away. I trusted to Medley and the doctor, who were on shore, to help me. My aim was to get hold of the men before they were too tipsy to move. Going up the river we landed at Donna Anna's, where I found Medley, and together we hastened on to Tumbez. On the way we fell in with our doctor, M'Cabe. We told him our object.

"I'll manage it for you," he said. "I'll frighten them out of their wits, and make them ready enough to return on board. I'll just hint to them that the liquor is poisoned, and so it is, for it's poison itself. They saw how the other watch looked when they came back, more dead than alive, and they'll be ready enough to believe me. I'll go on first, and then do you come up, and we'll get them down to the boat before they've time to think about it."

We agreed, and the doctor hurried on. We followed slowly. On arriving at the town we found some of the men already half-seas over, and the rest looking very much scared at what the doctor had told them. Some proposed attacking the place, and burning it down in revenge, but we suggested that they would be better employed in carrying their helpless ship-mates to the boats, that they might be the sooner under the doctor's care. The wine-shop keepers and their friends, afraid of losing their prey, did their utmost to prevent this, but we succeeded, and half-carrying half-dragging, we got the tipsy men down to the boats. The doctor observing that exercise was the best thing to keep off the effects of the poison, the more sober willingly took to the oars, and to the surprise of the captain we soon made our appearance alongside. The doctor took good care to dose all hands round, and though several were very ill from the effects of the abominable aguadente, he got the credit of saving their lives.

The captain, having no excuse for not sailing, gave the order to weigh at daybreak. The question was in what direction we should steer? Should we go back to the Galapagos, look into their harbours, and cruise about those islands? It was not likely that the mate of the "Lady Alice," after losing his captain, would remain long in that neighbourhood when all hope of finding him had been abandoned. Captain Bland thought that he would go either to the Marquesas or Sandwich Islands, to obtain hands, without whom he could not prosecute the object of the voyage.

"Then what will your wife and daughter do?" asked Captain Hake. "Will they remain on board, or take a passage home in the first full ship they fall in with?"

"They will remain on board the 'Lady Alice,

I feel sure of that," said Captain Bland, in a tone of confidence. "They'll not give me up so quickly. They'll think that I have got on board some ship, or landed on one of the islands, or have come across to the mainland. Women do not give up those they love in the way indifferent persons are apt to do. They'll not believe I am lost, but oh! how terribly anxious they'll be, notwithstanding, poor dears, poor dears!" and my kind friend hid his face in his hands to conceal his grief.

I had all the time the thought in my mind of that abominable schooner with her miscreant crew, and the terrible dread that she might have fallen in with the "Lady Alice" while her boats were away, and run off with her. What resistance could the five or six people left on board offer, even though they might have suspected her character before she got up to them? Still, I had the wisdom to keep these thoughts to myself.

The captains decided on sailing first for the Galapagos, and then to the Marquesas and Sandwich Islands, calling off all intermediate islands. They hoped, also, to fall in with other whalers from whom information might be obtained. Scarcely had we got out of the bay than the wind headed us, and we were making a long board to the southward, when the sound of a gun was heard. It was followed by several others in quick succession. The reports evidently came from the direction in which we were sailing. Instead of tacking, as the captain had intended to do, he stood on. I went aloft with a glass, and in a short time I saw two vessels standing off from the land on the opposite tack to that we were holding. The leading vessel was a schooner, the other a large ship, which was firing her bow-chasers at her. I could see the puffs of smoke issuing from the bows of the ship before I heard the reports. Every now and then the chase fired a stern-gun, for the purpose, I guessed, of trying to knock away some of her pursuer's spars, though from the distance they were apart it seemed to me with very little chance of success. The schooner showed no colours, but presently I saw a flag fly out from the peak of the ship, which, though indistinct, I was nearly sure was that of the Peruvian Republic. That the schooner was the dreaded craft which had so long haunted my imagination I felt perfectly certain, as I was that her piratical character was known, and that the man-of-war was intent on her capture. Still, there seemed a possibility of her escaping should her pursuer not succeed in winging her. We might, however, cut her off, and prevent her from getting away. I watched the two vessels for a few minutes longer, and then hurried down on deck to tell Captain Hake what I had seen, and to suggest to him that we might enable the man-of-war to capture the schooner.

"What business have we to interfere with the quarrels of foreigners?" he remarked. "The chase is probably a smuggler, which has been trying to land her cargo on the coast, or it may be has some refugees on board belonging to one of the many parties who are always at logger-heads."

"But, sir, I am morally certain that she is the schooner we saw off the Galapagos, to which those ruffians who attacked us belonged," I exclaimed. "Perhaps she has been plundering some English vessel, and for what we can tell she may have fallen in with the 'Lady Alice.'"

I felt constrained to say this to induce Captain Hake to do as I proposed, I did not stop to consider the effect it might produce on Captain Bland.

"Jack may be right," he exclaimed, in an agitated tone. "My good friend, don't hesitate to follow his suggestion. If we make one tack to the north-west, and then put about again we shall cross her bows, when it will be hard if we cannot knock away some of her spars; or perhaps when her crew see what we are about, they'll lower their sails to save themselves from worse consequences.'

Captain Hake made no reply; but, to my great satisfaction, at once put the ship about, and soon afterwards ordered the guns to be loaded and the muskets to be brought on deck. He was a man of deeds rather than of words. Captain Bland thanked him heartily.

"We must see that we are not making fools of ourselves before you need do that," he answered, somewhat gruffly.

We stood on for some time, and then again put about. After this we rapidly approached the schooner, which had lately been drawing ahead of the corvette. The latter had ceased firing, but was crowding on more sail. Once more we put about so as to be on the same course as the schooner. Captain Hake had been narrowly scanning her; as we got her within range he went to one of the guns, Captain Bland took charge of another, the mate of a third, and I, no one interfering, prepared to fire the fourth, all run out at the same side. We were now well to windward, all our guns pointed high. The captain, ordering the man at the helm to luff up, fired; the rest of us in succession followed his example. Our crew gave a hearty cheer, for the schooner's main gaff was shot away, and the next moment down came her fore-topmast, the square topsail hanging over the side and the jib trailing in the water. Our work was done, and we stood on. In a short time the corvette was almost close alongside the schooner, into which she at once poured her broadside. I fancied that I could hear the shrieks and groans of the hapless crew as the shot swept across the deck of the chase, or crashed into her side, and the sound of the rending and tearing of the stout planks. The pirates had had the madness to fire at the Government cruiser when all hope of escape was gone.

We were by this time away to leeward, and on the point of heaving-to, the corvette being the nearest to us. Beyond her I could see the masts of the schooner; they were bending over away from her antagonist. For a few seconds my attention was drawn from her, as I had to assist in bracing round the yards; when I looked again the masts had disappeared, the corvette was standing on also, about to brace round her head yards—the schooner had sunk with every human being on board. We saw no boat lowered to attempt saving the lives of any who might be still floating on the surface. Perhaps none were seen.

Captain Bland, hoping that he might possibly obtain some information about the "Lady Alice" on board the corvette at once borrowed a boat and invited me to accompany him to visit her. He was remarkably silent as we pulled for the ship, and thus my mind had time to recur to the gloomy thoughts which had before pained me so much.

"What if on board that schooner there were others than her crew—prisoners taken from any vessel they might have pillaged? All had shared the common fate, and I had been instrumental in their destruction. What if the pirates had, as I dreaded, attacked the 'Lady Alice and carried off Mrs. Bland and Mary?" The idea was too terrible; I tried to put it away from me. Perhaps the same thought was causing anguish to the heart of my friend. I was thankful when we got alongside the corvette; our fears would be relieved, or we might know the worst. The accommodation ladder was lowered and manned to do us honour, and the captain, an Englishman by his appearance, stood ready to receive us. He put out his hand as Captain Bland stepped on deck, and warmly greeted him.

"I am deeply obliged, captain, for the service you have rendered me in knocking away that rascally schooner's spars," he said in a frank tone.

G

"She might have got off otherwise, and given me another long cruise in search of her. I have been on the look-out for the villains for months past ; for they have plundered numerous vessels, and sunk or destroyed others I suspect, besides pillaging the villages along the coast. I should have been glad to have taken them alive to have had them tried, but our shot made more sure work than I expected."

"Can you tell me, sir, the names of the English vessels the pirates are supposed to have plundered ?" asked Captain Bland in an agitated tone.

"If we are to believe the stories current at the Peruvian ports, I should say half-a-dozen at least," answered the captain. "Let me see, there is the 'Ruby,' the 'Jane and John' the 'Lady Alice,' the——

"Good heavens, sir!" cried Captain Bland, interrupting him. "Were the people on board ill-treated ? Did the ruffians take any of them away, or did they merely carry off such valuables and stores and provisions as they could lay hands on ?"

"The 'Lady Alice' are you speaking of?" asked the captain in a tone which showed that he did not suppose we were interested in her fate. "By the bye, though they attacked her they did not succeed in getting on board, for they were driven off in the most gallant fashion by her crew, notwithstanding that her captain and several hands were away in a boat, and it is much feared have been lost."

"Thank heaven," ejaculated Captain Bland. "Blessings on my brave fellows. I am her captain, sir. Can you tell me where she is? Are my wife and daughter well?"

"She is safe enough in the port of Payta, I hope, by this time, as we convoyed her within a few leagues of the harbour, and then stood away in search of the schooner which has just met her just doom. Your wife and daughter, to whom I paid a visit on board, were well, and though anxious about you, persisted in believing that you would be restored to them."

"I knew that they would never give me up for lost. They have been spared much misery, anxious as they may have been. Thank heaven for that!" cried my kind friend, grasping the captain's hand. "I am grateful to you, sir, for the good news you have given me, indeed I am; and now, with your leave, I'll return on board the 'Eagle,' that we may get to Payta as soon as possible."

Though the captain of the corvette politely pressed us to stop for dinner, and offered to send for Captain Hake, I was glad that Captain Bland declined his proposals. Directly we got on board, the boat being hoisted in, we made sail for Payta, where we shortly arrived. The appearance of Captain Bland and his boat's crew caused no little astonishment on board the "Lady Alice," for both officers and men had given them up for lost. I went into the cabin to break the news to Mrs. Bland and Mary. They guessed at once by my countenance that Captain Bland had returned. He quickly followed me. " I knew that you would come back, father. I was sure that God would take care of you," exclaimed Mary, as, half weeping and half laughing, she clung round his neck. How blessed it is to possess a perfect confidence in our Heavenly Father's protecting care over those we love!

CHAPTER VI.

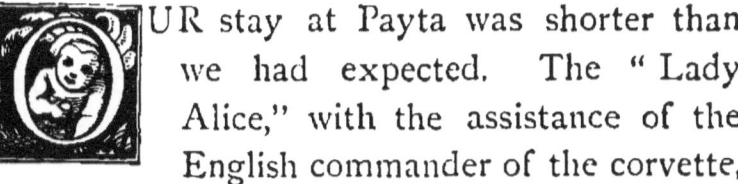UR stay at Payta was shorter than we had expected. The " Lady Alice," with the assistance of the English commander of the corvette, obtained more speedily than would otherwise have been the case all the repairs she required, and Captain Bland secured several good hands from among the crew of a merchantman wrecked further down the coast. Captain Hake gave the larboard watch of our ship leave on shore to make amends for their disappointment at Tumbez, but they did no credit to our country, for after quarrelling with the natives, during which one of them was stabbed, they were brought off in the last stage of brutal intoxication, from which it took them several days to recover.

I paid frequent visits to the " Lady Alice," which lay close alongside us. Captain Hake. did not object to my doing that, but when Captain Bland again asked him for the loan of me (as he put it) my captain assumed the glummest of glum looks, and replied, " I thought that I had settled that matter before. The lad came out in this ship, and he goes home in her, if I have my will."

Though disappointed when Captain Bland told me this I had much reason to be thankful that I was able to enjoy, even at intervals, the civilising influences of female society. How different my lot to that of many poor lads away for four long years from any one who takes the slightest interest in their moral welfare, or attempts to raise their minds above the grovelling existence of their brutal associates. I should be ungrateful if I did not mention, in addition to other advantages, the benefit I derived from the society of Medley, who was truly a friend to be prized.

It was a great consolation to me to find that the two ships were to cruise in company, though I might possibly not be able for many weeks together to visit the " Lady Alice." On leaving Payta we steered westward for the usual cruising ground. We had each at the end of ten days taken a couple of whales, when one Sunday morning a number appeared in different directions. The " Eagle's " boats were quickly in chase, but those of the " Lady Alice " remained hanging from the davits.

"What can the old man be about?" I heard the captain remark to the first mate as they were about to shove off. "It cannot be that he doesn't see the whales. The owners will be down upon him if he doesn't look after their interests better."

He said something to the same effect as he passed under our consort's stern.

"I keep the ten commandments, Captain Hake," answered Captain Bland. "The Master who gave them is the greatest of the two, and He will look after the owners' interests."

By night on that occasion our boats had brought two whales alongside, but the crews were so weary from having been away all day under a scorching sun that they were unable to commence cutting in till next morning. At that time the boats of the "Lady Alice" were away, and in less than an hour had brought one whale alongside; shortly afterwards another was secured, so that as it turned out both ships commenced trying out at the same time, and the "Lady Alice" had the whole of the oil stowed away by Saturday night. The same sort of thing occurred more than once after this. Captain Bland adhered to his rule, and by the end of the week had stowed as many barrels of oil in his hold as we had.

At length whales becoming scarce, the two captains agreed to proceed westward across the Pacific to the Japan whaling ground. We called off various islands on our way, chiefly to obtain fresh provisions and water. At length we reached the neighbourhood of the Kingsmill group, off which we found so many whales that we remained for several months, during which time we captured a large number. As there is no safe anchorage the ships had to stand off and on while the boats went on shore to obtain water and provisions, but we had to be very careful in our dealings with the natives, who were thorough savages and treacherous in the extreme.

The weather now gave signs of changing, but as every day a whale was seen the captains were tempted to remain on. I had of late frequently gone away in the boats, generally with Medley, who had become a good harpooner. For two days not a whale had been seen, and we were on the point of proceeding further west when about noon a whole school appeared, and scattering sported far and wide over the surface of the deep. All the boats from both ships were lowered, and I went in one with Medley, who was intent on attacking a large whale which we saw to the eastward, in which direction the land lay from us. Just as we had got within a dozen fathoms of the monster up went its flukes and it sounded, leaving us looking very blank at the spot where it had gone down.   It might be forty minutes or more before it would come up again.   We determined to wait, and as we had had a sharp pull we refreshed ourselves by munching some biscuits and drinking a part of the contents of our water breaker.   The whale remained down a much longer time than we had expected, and when it came up appeared far away to the eastward, or much closer to the shore.   Again we bent to our oars, eager to get fast before it should once more sound.   It was as much as we should do to reach it in time; if we were too late we should scarcely have another chance before dark.

Already the sun was hidden by a dark bank of clouds rising above the horizon, and the wind was blowing strong from the westward, but pulling directly before it we did not feel its force, though it was evident that the sea was gradually getting up.   I could see both the ships at some distance apart, but none of the boats were visible to us sitting down.   I ought to have told Medley, who, having his eye on the whale ahead, did not remark the change in the weather.   "If we kill the whale we shall be able to lie made fast under its lee, even should it come on to blow, till the 'Eagle' can come and pick us up," I thought. The whale, after remaining so long under water, took a proportionate time to spout on the surface. We were close to it. Medley, making a sign to the bow oarsman to take his place, stepped forward and stood up harpoon in hand. We ceased pulling—the next instant a loud thud showed us that the weapon had struck deep into the monster's side. He followed up the blow by plunging in three lances, and was about to hurl a fourth when he shouted out "Back off all!" while he allowed the line to run rapidly out of the tub over the bollard. We backed our oars with all our might, knowing that our lives might depend on our getting clear of the monster before it commenced the fearful struggles it was probably about to make. Instead of sounding, however, or lashing the water with its flukes, it darted off along the surface at a rapid rate towards the land. Already a considerable portion of the line had run out when Medley secured it round the bollard, and away we flew, towed by the whale, at a furious rate through the water The second line was secured to the end of the first, in case the whale should suddenly sound; but this it seemed to have no intention of doing. On and on we were dragged farther and farther from the ships, but we had no thoughts of cutting loose from the whale after all our exertions, and we hoped that, in its endeavours to escape, it would wear out its strength, and thus become an easy prey. Medley stood ready all the time to slacken out more line should its speed become so great as to run the risk of its dragging the bows under water, while the man next him sat with axe in hand prepared to cut it in case there was a probability of the boat being swamped. Nearer and nearer we approached the land, till we could distinctly see the surf rising up in a wall of foam, and breaking over the coral reef surrounding it. We expected every moment that the whale would turn to avoid the danger ahead, and that we should be able to haul in the slack of the rope, and get sufficiently close to give it another wound. That it was losing blood, and consequently its strength, we knew by the red tinge of the water in its wake; still it held on. I glanced towards the shore—I could see a gap in the line of surf, beyond which the land rose to a greater height than anywhere near. It formed, I concluded, the entrance to a bay or lagoon, but seemed so narrow that even a boat would run the danger of being swamped by the surging waters on either side. Galled or terror-stricken as the whale evidently was, I could scarcely suppose that it would run itself on shore, yet from the course it was taking it seemed possible that such it was about to do. Suddenly, however, the roar of the surf growing louder and louder, it appeared to perceive its danger, and leaping almost out of the water it turned away to the northward, giving the boat so violent a jerk that she was nearly capsized. Escaping that danger, we were exposed to another, for the sea, now brought on our beam, continually broke over the side, employing two hands in baling, while often it appeared as if she would be turned completely over. At length the monster began to lessen its speed, and we were hauling in the line to get up to it, when suddenly raising its flukes down it went, dragging out the line again at a rate which made the bollard smoke, but the sea breaking over the bows prevented it from catching fire. The first line was soon drawn out—the second went on, and that, too, speedily ran towards the end. It was vain to attempt stopping it. The whale was now, we knew, swimming under water, and heading away from the shore. It must ere long come up again—but could we hold on till then?

Already the seas broke fearfully over the bows. In spite of the efforts of the men baling, the boat was half full of water. Medley seized the axe; the bitter end of the last line was reached. A dark sea came rolling on. Nothing could save us from being swamped, it seemed. The axe descended, a loud thud was heard, the line was severed. "Back off all!" cried Medley, taking the bow oar to steer by. We pulled for our lives; the sea broke under the bows. Scarcely till now were we conscious that, after all our toils, the whale was lost. We had not, as we had hoped, its huge body to hang on to, to protect us from the fury of the fast-rising seas. Darkness had now come on; we looked out in vain for either of the ships. The "Eagle," on finding that we did not return, would burn blue lights to direct us to her. The "Lady Alice" would do the same should any of her boats be absent. We pulled on against the still rising seas. How long our boat would float amid them was doubtful. "There's a light, boys!" cried Medley at length; but it was away to the northward, and far off, for it only just appeared above the horizon. To reach it we must bring the sea abeam and run a fearful risk of being rolled over or swamped. Still the attempt must be made, unless we were prepared to remain toiling at the oars all night, or to run the risk of trying to reach the shore. We continued to pull on, keeping the boat's head to the sea, when, looking round, I observed a glimmering bluish light suddenly spring up on the starboard bow. That it was at an immense distance I knew, as I could not distinguish the body from which the rays of light proceeded. Medley saw it also. "She is hull down, and it would take us till morning to reach her, even if we could do it then," he said in a tone which showed how serious he thought our condition. Still we could more easily reach the vessel from which the distant light proceeded than the one on our beam.

Our situation was sufficient to alarm the stoutest hearts, and we were all young and comparatively inexperienced. The dark sky seemed to have come down close above our heads; the foam-covered seas came rolling on, every instant increasing in size, while astern was the dreadful reef, over which the furious breakers were dashing with a terrific roar. I had given up my oar to another man, and was seated near Medley, when I saw a small bright speck in the sky just above the horizon.

"What is that? Can it come from a ship?" I asked, pointing it out to him. He was silent. Gradually the spot of light expanded into an arch.

"It is the eye of an hurricane," he said at length. "We shall have it break upon us presently, and if we fail to reach the land, Jack, we shall not live to see another sunrise."

Calmly telling the men to be prepared for the worst, but not to despair, he put the boat round, and we pulled in for the land. I told him of the opening I had seen. He had observed it also, but was doubtful whether we should discover it in the darkness. Still, unless we could do so, our destruction seemed certain. Earnestly I prayed for deliverance; so did Medley, I know. With fearful rapidity, borne onward by the sea, we approached the raging breakers. For some time in vain we looked along the line of foam for the opening we had seen. The howling tempest astern forbade us attempting to pull off the shore; but should we gain it, if it was inhabited, what sort of treatment were we to expect from the savages? Several boats' crews had, it was said, lost their lives among this group. I was straining my eyes ahead when I made out against the sky the outline of the high land I had before remarked. Beyond it the clouds appeared to be brighter than in any other part of the heavens. The instant afterwards the pale moon burst forth, and though but for a brief space, it was long enough to enable her to serve as a beacon to us. Directly below her we saw the looked-for opening.

"Give way, lads, we may yet save our lives,' cried Medley.

The men did give way, but so narrow appeared the opening that it seemed impossible we should get through without being swamped by the breakers rising high up on either side, rendered visible and more terrific by the vivid flashes of lightning darting from the clouds, which were followed by crashing peals of thunder, sounding above even the roaring of the angry waters. Onwards we were carried, the foam leaping high above our heads on the summit of a hissing sea, and then down we shot like an arrow, guided by Medley's oar, on to the comparatively calm surface of a deep bay. A few strokes more we glided up it, and were in smooth water, the moon not hiding her face till we were in safety. We made out before us a sandy beach, towards which we steered, and, leaping out, drew up our boat to free her of water.

Our first act was to kneel down and return thanks to our Heavenly Father, who had so mercifully preserved us, and most of our rough crew, though at first they hesitated, followed our example. We then looked out for a place which would afford us shelter during the night from the raging storm. Near the beach was a grove of palm-trees, but the wind, howling amid their stems, bent and twisted them about so furiously that we had reason to dread, should we lie down under them, that some, being uprooted, might fall and crush us. Keeping outside the trees, we made our way towards the high ground, one side of which we found consisted of a coral cliff, and we had not searched long before we discovered a cave large enough to afford shelter to all our party. The floor was of sand, and having no fear of venomous creatures or savage beasts, the men threw themselves down to obtain the rest they all so much required. We had brought from the boat the biscuits and the small stock of water we possessed, but none of them were inclined to eat, though they drank up more than half the quantity of the precious liquid remaining in the breaker. Medley and I, who, as were the rest, wet to the skin, walked up and down under shelter of the rock trying to dry our clothes.

" If we had but a fire it would be a great comfort," I observed.

Pepper, one of our Kroomen, hearing what I said, exclaimed, " Massa, me got light, nebber fear!" Groping about, he soon found two pieces of dry wood, and fashioning them with his knife, he began to rub one against the other in a way which at length produced a bright spark. I had a handful of leaves ready, and we had quickly a capital fire blazing up just inside the cave.   How grateful we felt for its genial warmth !

What if, while we were congratulating ourselves on being safe on shore, any misfortune should happen to those in whom we were so deeply interested ?   I felt that I would thankfully be on board the "Lady Alice" to share the fate of my friends, or to aid, as far as human strength could go, in averting the danger to which they might be exposed.   I knew, however, that my wishes were of no avail.   I knelt down with Medley, and prayed with all earnestness that they might be protected ; we then stretched ourselves on the sand near our men.

"Jack, it did not occur to me before that this island may be inhabited ; if so, that our fire may attract the natives," said Medley, just as I was dropping off to sleep.   "It ought to be put out, or we must keep watch.   They might murder us before we could attempt to defend ourselves."

I agreed with him, but confessed that I could no longer keep my eyes open.

"I'll keep the first watch, and then I'll call up Pepper and Salt, and the latter shall call you. The others cannot be depended on," he said, though I could scarcely comprehend the meaning of his words.

It was nearly daylight when Salt at last awoke me. He would not have done so then, honest fellow, had not he been ordered. I asked him if he had heard or seen any natives.

"No, Massa Jack, me tink none here; but better get to de boat and catch some fish for breakfast, and den if any savage come we ready to start," he answered.

I thought his advice good, and desired him, as soon as it was light, to go down to the boat and get the lines ready, so that we might shove off as soon as the other men awoke. I, in the meantime, directly the dawn broke, made my way to the summit of the hill, that I might survey the island, and, if possible, ascertain the position of the ships. I had fortunately brought a small but powerful telescope given me by Captain Bland. The fury of the hurricane was over, but the breakers still beat with violence against the barrier reef, and made it impossible for us to put to sea. In a short time the glorious sun, rising above the horizon amid the fast dispersing clouds, shed a bright light over sea and land, and enabled me to obtain a far-extending view.

The island on which we had taken refuge was much smaller than I had supposed, owing to the reef which extended along it; but across a narrow passage was another of much greater extent and away to the north and north-west were several others, besides numerous reefs marked by the white masses of foam flying over them. Several tiny wreaths of smoke which rose up amid the groves on the nearest island showed me that that, at all events, was inhabited, as, probably, were most of the others. As the mist of morning cleared away I could distinguish in the distance the huts of the natives, though, owing probably to the barren nature of the soil at the end nearest our island, none were built there.

Again and again I swept the horizon in search of the ships; nowhere could I discern them. In what direction could they have been driven? I at last observed beyond a line of reefs what I took to be a group of cocoa-nut trees rising out of a low islet faintly traced against the blue sky like gossamer webs. Yes, there were trees, but among them, after keeping my glass steady for a minute or more, I made out the masts and yards of a ship. That she was either the "Eagle" or the "Lady Alice" I felt certain, but how she had escaped the reefs and been driven in where I saw her I could not conjecture. As her masts appeared upright I trusted that she was not on shore; but whether such were the case or not, she might find it difficult to escape from her position should the savage inhabitants of the neighbouring shores try to make her their prey, as they had succeeded in doing other vessels under similar circumstances. What was even now going forward on board her, who could tell? Again I looked round in vain for the other ship, and then hastened down to join Medley. I found him setting off with the other men for the boat, he supposing that I had gone with Salt to look after her. He could not even conjecture which of the ships I had seen, but he agreed with me that we must put off to try and get on board her the moment we could venture out to sea. He would have gone back with me to the hill, but the men were crying out for food, and insisting on endeavouring to catch some fish. None of the trees near us bore cocoa-nuts, nor had any water been found, probably the reason that the island was uninhabited.

Medley served only a small portion of biscuit to each man, and warned them all to be very careful of the water, as we might be unable to obtain more till we reached the ship. Judging by the surf which still beat furiously on the reef there was small prospect of our doing that till the next day at soonest. Salt had got the lines and hooks ready, and some shell-fish for bait, so we at once pulled out as near the entrance of the lagoon as we could venture. We had not had our lines down long before we began to get bites, and in a short time we had hauled in as many fish as would give us an ample supply of food for the day, we returned to the shore to cook and eat our prey. We again lighted a fire at the mouth of our cave, hoping that the smoke would not be seen by the savages, but to prevent being surprised Medley sent Pepper to the other side of the island to give us due warning should he see any of them coming over.

After breakfast the rest of the men lay down to sleep, while Medley and I went to the top of the hill to ascertain by the state of the sea when there was a probability of our getting off, and to watch for the appearance of the other ship. We looked for her in vain. The ocean, however, was rapidly losing the quickness of its motion, though the huge waves were still slowly and lazily tumbling against each other as they rolled on till they reached the reef, where, with a roar of thunder, they broke into masses of foam. The chief object of interest, the distant ship, remained motionless as before, her canvas closely furled. Had a sail been loosed we should have seen it fluttering in the breeze.

"In a few hours at most we shall be able to pass through yonder channel," observed Medley, pointing to the entrance of the lagoon. "Look, the sea scarcely even now breaks across it. If necessary, I would not hesitate to take out a boat in spite of the risk I might run ; but we will not make the attempt for the present."

I agreed with him that it would be folly to do so, and we returned to the cave. We sat down in the shade. The heat was great, and neither of us having had much rest, we both fell as sound asleep as were our men stretched at their lengths a short distance from us. Hours may have passed. I was aroused by Pepper shouting, " De savage come ! de savage come ! Quick, quick ! rouse up, boys, get to de boat."

Salt was the first to start to his feet on hearing his companion's voice, and by kicks and pulls to awaken the rest. I grasped Medley by the arm and helped him up. The men in a panic were hurrying off, when he reminded them of the breaker of water and the remainder of the fish which had fortunately been cooked. They took the breaker and fish up between them, and set off, while we waited for Pepper. He had seen a large body of savages, flourishing their formidable spears and gesticulating wildly, come down to the shore and begin to swim across the channel, evidently, as he supposed, having discovered that strangers were on the island, though how they had done so it was difficult to guess, unless they had seen Medley and me on the top of the hill. That they had hostile intentions was pretty evident by the account Pepper gave us. Had we possessed fire-arms we might have defended our selves, but as it was we could secure our safety alone by flight.

We found the men hurriedly launching the boat. In their dread of the savages I am not sure that they would have waited for us had we been delayed. The boat was quickly in the water, and we all leaped on board. Medley took the steering oar, and the men gave way. As I looked ahead I could see the green billows rolling in towards the opening, and still breaking with fearful force against the barrier reef on either side, but in the centre I observed a clear glass-like swell, over which I hoped we might find a safe passage. Medley seemed not quite certain about the matter, and told the men to lay on their oars till he could perceive a favourable opportunity for dashing out. Just then a fearful yell sounded in our ears, and looking astern I saw the beach covered by a band of savages flourishing their spears and gesticulating to us to return and be killed. Some of the more active were springing along the rocks so as to get near enough to hurl their weapons at us.

The crew, without waiting for Medley's orders, bent to their oars, and though several spears fell into the water at no great distance off, we were soon beyond their reach. Without waiting to ascertain what the savages were about we steered for the centre of the passage. A sea like a mass of liquid malachite came rolling in—we mounted to its summit, and then descending into the trough, were soon rising on another watery height. The crew pulled lustily, and in a few minutes we were well outside the breakers, and able to turn the boat's head to the northward. It had become a perfect calm, so that we had a long pull before us. At this the men grumbled, as they had expected to hoist the sail. Medley, however, reminded them that had there been wind the ship would probably have got under weigh, and we should have missed her. We pulled on along the coast of the larger island, but whether or not we were perceived by the people on shore we could not tell. The men at last complaining of fatigue, declared that they must stop and take some food and water. To this Medley could not object, eager as he and I were to get up to the ship.

While the men were eating the remainder of the fish and biscuit, we kept two of the oars going, and had just passed a point forming one side of a bay when, looking towards the shore, we saw a fleet of large canoes, thirty or more, ranged along the shore, the people apparently hurrying on board. On examining them through my glass I perceived that they were all armed, and it at once occurred to me that they were starting on an expedition to attack the ship. Medley was of the same opinion.

"You see the savages in those boats," he exclaimed ; "let us see what you can do. If they catch us we shall be in their try pots before many hours have gone by, but if we can get on board the ship we can at all events have a fight for our lives."

The men needing no further incentive to exertion, cramming their food into their mouths, threw out their oars and away we flew over the now calm surface of the ocean. As I looked over the starboard quarter I saw that several of the canoes had shoved off from the beach and were coming after us. Had there been a breeze we should have had no chance of escaping them. In a short time the whole fleet was after us. The savages probably reckoned on our not knowing the shortest passages through the reefs, but Medley and I kept a bright look-out, I making a good use of my telescope. Now we had the coral rocks rising close to us. Several times I could see the bottom as we dashed on. Occasionally we had to turn either to the east or west, but still we were rapidly nearing the ship. My chief fear was that other canoes might be waiting further to the north and dash out upon us.

While standing up I brought my glass to bear on the ship. How thankful I felt when I became certain that she was the " Lady Alice." She had at all events escaped any accident from the hurricane, and I had no doubt that we should beat off the savages should they venture to attack her. Looking astern I saw to my satisfaction that we were greatly distancing the canoes, so that we should have time after getting on board to make preparations for their reception. At length we were discovered by our friends on board, for we saw several persons waving signals of welcome to us from the forecastle. Greatly to my relief also I saw that the ship was at anchor at some distance from the shore, while beyond her to the north-west the sea appeared free from reefs. Captain Bland shook my hand heartily.

" We had given you up for lost," he said ; " we heard that you were away from your ship when the hurricane came on, and that there was no chance of your getting on board her."

"How could you hear that?" I asked, much surprised.

"From the second mate and his crew, whom we took on board. Very glad I was to have them, as they were of the greatest assistance during the gale, though I fear Captain Hake must have been hard put to it without them."

I interrupted my old friend by telling him of the approach of the canoes. He was not a man to disregard a warning. The boarding nettings were at once triced up, the small arms got from below, and the guns loaded. I inquired anxiously for Mary and her mother, who were not on deck.

"They suffered much during the hurricane, but are now on foot, and will be glad to see you," answered the captain.

I sprang below. I should have startled my friends not a little had not the steward told them that I had come on board, for they had heard of the supposed loss of our boat, though Mary told me with a smile, while a tear was in her eye, that as her dear father had been preserved, so she had not despaired of again seeing me. I felt very happy, for I was sure that we should beat off the savages. On my return on deck I found that they had not yet appeared. It was now getting dark. This made us suspect that they had intended to attempt surprising the ship at night,

and very probably they would have succeeded
had we not providentially seen them and thus
been the means of putting our friends on their
guard. Captain Bland, always anxious to avoid
bloodshed, ordered the guns to be fired at
intervals, both to show the savages that we were
on the alert and to attract the attention of the
" Eagle " should she be in the neighbourhood.
Though prepared we could not avoid being
anxious, for if the natives were resolved on our
destruction we should have a severe struggle
before we could drive them off.

It had now become so dark that it would be
difficult to see the canoes till they were close to
us. All hands, therefore, remained on deck with
our weapons in our hands to be ready at a
moment's notice, but the hours went by, the
savages had thought better of it we hoped, and
dawn at length appeared. We looked out for
the canoes, but they were nowhere to be seen,
nor was the " Eagle." The calm continued, and
as we had our two boats besides those of the
" Lady Alice," Captain Bland resolved to tow
her out to sea so as to get a good offing before
another night. The anchor was hove up, and
with six boats ahead we made good progress.
We had got a couple of miles away from the
anchorage, and were nearly free of the reefs,

when the look-out at the masthead shouted that he saw the canoes coming towards us.

"Keep to your oars, lads," cried Captain Bland ; "we shall have a breeze presently, and shall then easily tackle them."

On came the canoes. It seemed too likely that they would reach us before the wished-for breeze had sprung up. The crews of the boats gave way lustily. I had remained on board. As I looked astern I fancied that I could almost hear the shrieks and shouts of the savages as they approached. Suddenly I saw the dog-waves blowing out. I, with the rest on board, sprang aloft to loose sails, the boats were called alongside, and by the time they were hoisted up we were gliding rapidly through the water. Though several of the canoes, hoisting their sails, got near us, a few shot, which carried away the masts of two or three, made them give up the pursuit, and in a few hours we had run the island out of sight.

We cruised in the neighbourhood of the group for two weeks or more in search of the "Eagle," but at last despairing of falling in with her continued on for the Japan whaling ground. Here being very successful, we got a full ship, and, to the joy of all on board, steered home-wards by way of the Indian seas, calling, how-

ever, at several interesting places to obtain fresh
provisions and water.

The white cliffs of old England were seen at
length, and home was reached. Captain Bland,
having made a successful voyage, declared that
he would never more tempt the ocean or expose
his wife and daughter to dangers such as those
from which they had been so mercifully preserved. The "Eagle" had not arrived, and
nothing was heard of her for several years, when
a report reached me that she had sought shelter
in one of the harbours of the group, when part of
the crew being on shore were set upon and
massacred, while those on board were overpowered and killed. The ship then having been
plundered was sunk with her cargo of oil, and
was thus found by another whaler the following
year through information given by one of the
natives.

Thus ended the voyages of the two whalers,
of which I have given of necessity but a hurried
sketch. I left the whaling service, and sooner
than I might have expected, obtained the com-
mand of a fine trader to China and the Eastern
seas, having the happiness of being accompanied by my dear Mary, who had become my
wife. My excellent friend Medley was equally
successful, and both of us having retired from

the sea, have settled near each other, and often spin to attentive young listeners the preceding yarn, and many others descriptive of our nautical career, though our boys and girls unanimously give the preference to the voyages of the Two Whalers.

THE END.

LONDON:
PRINTED BY JAS. TRUSCOTT & SON,
Suffolk Lane, City.

PUBLICATIONS

OF THE

Society for Promoting Christian Knowledge.

Most of these Works may be had in Ornamental Bindings, with Gilt Edges, at a small Extra charge.

Adventurous Voyage of the "Polly," and other Yarns.
By the late S. W. SADLER, R.N. With four page illustrations. Crown 8vo.................................*cloth boards*   3   0

All is Lost save Honour.
A Story of to-day. By CATHERINE M. PHILLIMORE, With three page illustrations. Crown 8vo....*cloth boards*   1   6

Alone Among the Zulus.
By a PLAIN WOMAN. The Narrative of a Journey through the Zulu Country. With four page illustrations. Crown 8vo...*cloth boards*   1   6

An Innocent.
By S. M. SITWELL. With three page illustrations. Crown 8vo...*cloth boards*   1   6

Baron's Head (The).
By FRANCIS VYVIAN. With three page illustrations. Crown 8vo...*cloth boards*   2   6

Behind the Clouds.
A Story of Village Life. By GRACE HAMILTON. Printed on toned paper, with three page illustrations. Crown 8vo...*cloth boards*   2   0

Belfrey of St. Jude (The).
A Story by ESMÈ STUART, author of "Mimi." With three page illustrations. Crown 8vo............*cloth boards*   2   6

Bernard Hamilton, Curate of Stowe.
By MARY E. SHIPLEY. With four page illustrations. Crown 8vo. ....*cloth boards*   2   0

Brag and Holdfast.
By EADGYTH, author of "The Snow Fort," &c. With three page illustrations. Crown 8vo............*cloth boards*   1   6
21.6.88.]   [Crown 8vo.

s. d.

Captain Eva.
The Story of a Naughty Girl. By KATHLEEN KNOX. With three page illustrations. Crown 8vo. ...*cloth boards* 1 6

Chryssie's Hero.
By ANNETTE LYSTER, author of "Fan's Silken String." With three page illustrations. Crown 8vo....*cloth boards* 2 6

Christabel the Flower Girl of Covent Garden.
By the author of "Our Valley," &c. With three page illustrations. Crown 8vo...........................*cloth boards* 1 6

Cruise of the "Dainty," (The); or, Rovings in the Pacific.
By the late W. H. G. KINGSTON. With three page illustrations. Crown 8vo. ....*cloth boards* 1 6

Engel the Fearless.
By ELIZABETH H. MITCHELL. With four page illustrations. Crown 8vo. ....*cloth boards* 3 6

Fan's Silken String.
By ANNETTE LYSTER, author of "Northwind and Sunshine," &c. With three page illustrations. Crown 8vo. *cloth boards* 1 6

Fortunes of Hassan (The).
Being the strange story of a Turkish Refugee, as told by himself. By the author of "Our Valley," "Rosebuds." With three page illustrations. Crown 8vo....*cloth boards* 2 6

Frontier Fort (The); or Stirring Times in the North-West Territory of British America.
By the late W. H. G. KINGSTON. With three page illustrations. Crown 8vo.............................*cloth boards* 1 6

Geoffrey Bennett.
By Mrs. ISLA SITWELL, author of the "Church Farm. With three page wood cuts. Crown 8vo. ......*cloth boards* 3 0

Great Captain (The). An Eventful Chapter in Spanish History.
By ULICK R. BURKE, M.A. With two page illustrations. Crown 8vo.................................*cloth boards* 2 0

Hasselaers (The).
A Tale of Courage and endurance. By E. E. COOPER. With three page illustrations. Crown 8vo....*cloth boards* 1 6

s. d.

Invasion of Ivylands (The).
By ANNETTE LYSTER, author of "Fan's Silken String."
With three page illustrations. Crown 8vo. ...*cloth boards* 1 6

John Holbrook's Lessons.
By M. E. PALGRAVE. With three page illustrations.
Crown 8vo. ....*cloth boards* 1 6

King's Warrant (The).
A Tale of Old and New France. By A. H. ENGELBACH.
With three page illustrations. Crown 8vo. ...*cloth boards* 2 6

Lettice.
By Mrs. MOLESWORTH, author of "Carrots." With
three page illustrations. Crown 8vo............*cloth boards* 2 0

Little Brown Girl (The).
A Story for Children. By ESMÈ STUART, author of
" Mimi," &c. With three page illustrations. Crown 8vo.
cloth boards 2 6

Mate of the " Lily " (The); or, Notes from Harry Musgrave's Log Book.
By the late W. H. G. KINGSTON, author of "Owen
Hartley, &c., With three page illustrations. Crown 8vo.
cloth boards 1 6

Mike.
A Tale of the Great Irish Famine. By the Rev. E. N.
HOARE, M.A., author of "Between the Locks." With
three page illustrations. Crown 8vo............*cloth boards* 1 6

Mimi: a Story of Peasant Life in Normandy.
By ESMÈ STUART, author of " The Little Brown Girl."
With three page illustrations. Crown 8vo....*cloth boards* 2 6

Mrs. Dobbs' Dull Boy.
By ANNETTE LYSTER, author of " Northwind and Sunshine," &c. With three page illustrations. Crown 8vo.
cloth boards 2 6

My Lonely Lassie.
By ANNETTE LYSTER, author of " Mrs. Dobbs' Dull Boy."
With three page illustrations. Crown 8vo. ...*cloth boards* 2 6

Our Valley.
By the author of " The Children of Seeligsberg," &c.
With three page illustrations. Crown 8vo....*cloth boards* 2 6

Percy Trevor's Training.
By the Rev. E. N. HOARE, M.A., author of " Two
Voyages," &c. With three page illustrations. Crown 8vo.
cloth boards 2 6

LONDON: NORTHUMBERLAND AVENUE, CHARING CROSS, W.C.
43, QUEEN VICTORIA STREET, E.C.
BRIGHTON: 135, NORTH STREET.